HELP!
I'M TRAPPED IN MY
GYM TEACHER'S BODY

OTHER BOOKS BY TODD STRASSER

HELP!
I'M TRAPPED IN MY
GYM TEACHER'S BODY

TODD STRASSER

AN
APPLE
PAPERBACK

SCHOLASTIC INC.
New York Toronto London Auckland Sydney

To Emily and Elizabeth Rodney

The author would also like to thank the staff
and students of Hommocks Junior High School
for allowing him to snoop around.

ISBN 0-590-67987-2

12 11 10 9 8 7 6 5 4 3 2 1   6 7 8 9/9 0 1/0

Printed in the U.S.A.   40

First Scholastic printing, January 1996

1

"Here he comes," Julia Saks whispered.

Everyone at our lunch table looked up.

"What amazing muscles!" said Amber Sweeny. She was talking about our new gym teacher, Mr. Braun, who'd just entered the cafeteria. Because he was new that year, he'd gotten stuck with lunch duty.

"What a hunk," Julia said dreamily.

"What a *freak*," countered Josh Hopka. Mr. Braun was the most muscular person we'd ever seen in real life. His arms and chest bulged through his dark blue polo shirt, stretching the material tight. His neck was like a tree trunk and you could see the ripples in his stomach through his shirt.

"He's unnatural," I said.

"A freak o' nature," Andy Kent summed it up.

Josh and I smiled. We watched as Mr. Braun caught a glimpse of his reflection in a cafeteria window. He flexed his right arm, making the muscle bulge even more. I was certain his shirt sleeve was going to rip, but it didn't.

"Aw, my hero!" Alex Silver whispered in a high falsetto. The guys chuckled, but Julia Saks narrowed her big brown eyes at us.

"You're just jealous," she said.

"No way!" Josh insisted. "You think I'd want to be a musclehead? Forget it." He turned to me. "What about you, Jake?"

Instead of answering, I glanced over at Amber, who was still gazing at Mr. Braun. Amber had long, straight, brown hair and smooth flawless skin. She was really pretty.

"See?" Julia smiled knowingly. "Jake wouldn't mind looking like that."

Amber turned and caught me with her almond-shaped green eyes. I quickly looked away.

"Recent surveys show that big muscles are the number one cause of stupidity," Andy announced. He was using the end of a plastic straw to pick some gunk out of his braces.

"That's a good one," Amber giggled.

"I'm serious," Andy insisted. "The brain has to work so hard to control all those muscles that it doesn't have room to think."

Everyone scowled at him. Andy was tall with short black hair. He often said weird things. We never knew whether he was serious or not.

"You know what they say," I added. "Those

who can, do. Those who can't, teach. And those who can't teach, teach gym."

Amber laughed, revealing her straight white teeth. I felt good when I made her laugh.

"Watch this," Alex whispered to us. He waved his arm. "Hey, Mr. Braun!"

"What's up, Silver?" The gym teacher stepped up to our table and crossed his massive arms. He had a deep, husky voice and a square face with short black hair. It was only 11:30 in the morning, but his jaw was already darkened by stubble.

"How long does it take to grow all those muscles?" Alex asked innocently.

Josh sniggered silently. Andy covered his mouth with his hand and tried not to laugh. Mr. Braun didn't notice.

"I started lifting when I was fourteen," he replied. "Just about your age."

"How often?" Alex asked.

"Four or five days a week."

"Wow!" Alex pretended to be impressed. "How many hours a day?"

"Two or three at least."

We traded amazed looks. It was hard to imagine doing *anything* for two or three hours a day . . . except, maybe, watching TV.

"How come so much?" asked Alex.

"You have to work on all the major muscle groups," Mr. Braun explained. "It's not just hav-

3

ing big muscles. It's about symmetry and cuts."

"What's that?" Andy asked.

"Symmetry means having a balanced physique," Mr. Braun explained. "It looks bad if you have big pecs and no traps. Cuts mean muscle definition. You want to see each individual muscle."

"Oh, I get it." Alex gave an exaggerated nod. From the tone of his voice, we knew he was getting ready to deliver the zinger. "But here's the thing I don't get, Mr. Braun. How come you can't find any clothes that *fit*?"

2

Julia Saks looked away so Mr. Braun couldn't see her face. I bit down on my lip to keep from laughing out loud. Josh and Andy clamped their hands over their mouths and made funny, muffled noises as if they could hardly control themselves. Mr. Braun's face hardened and his eyes became beady. He'd just realized that Alex was goofing on him.

"This is the largest size this shirt comes in, Silver," he replied icily. He glared down at Alex and the red lunch tray in front of him. "French fries, chocolate pudding, and lemonade. Is that your *lunch?*"

"Uh huh." Alex grinned as if he were proud.

Mr. Braun raised a disdainful eyebrow. "That's what I call a real healthy diet, Silver."

I couldn't help chuckling. Unfortunately, Mr. Braun saw me. "What's so funny, Sherman?"

"Uh, nothing, Mr. Brain, er, I meant, Braun." It was an honest mistake, but everyone at the table stared at me.

"What is that *thing* on your tray?" Mr. Braun asked.

"A potato," I said. This year the school had added a potato bar at lunch.

"What's *on* it?"

"Melted cheese, pineapple, and bacon bits."

Mr. Braun made a face like he wanted to hurl, then shook his head in disgust. "You kids eat the worst garbage I've ever seen. I won't be surprised if your bodies fall apart by the time you're fifty."

"That's cool," Alex replied defiantly. "Life's over by then anyway."

"You won't feel that way in twenty-six years," Mr. Braun said.

3

After Mr. Braun left, Alex turned to us with a puzzled look on his face. "In twenty-six years I'll be forty, not fifty."

"He probably meant *thirty*-six years," Amber said.

"Yeah," I said, "then you'd be fifty."

Alex shook his head in disbelief. "Can't the guy *add*?"

"His brain doesn't have room to add," Andy said as he popped a couple of Skittles into his mouth. "It's too busy telling all those muscles what to do."

"Give it a rest, Andy," Julia groaned.

"Hey, talk about no room for brains." Josh looked up from the table. "Here comes Barry Dunn."

A chill went down my spine. Coming toward us was a big kid wearing a baggy green T-shirt and black jeans with white patches on the knees. His head was shaved almost completely bald, except for one long blond lock that grew from the back of his skull down between his shoulders. Earrings dangled from both ears. His deep-set eyes were focused directly on me.

"Better hide, Jake," Josh warned in a low voice. For some reason which no one understood, Barry Dunn hated me and picked on me constantly. If Amber hadn't been sitting at the table with us, I probably would have hidden. But I didn't want her to think I was chicken.

As Barry came closer, the kids at the tables around us grew quiet. Everyone in school was afraid of Barry. They all watched as he came around our table and stood behind me. I braced myself for a major knuckle noogy, or a super-painful shoulder tweak.

Instead, Barry bent down and growled into my ear. "Behind the garage in ten minutes."

"But it's cold out," I whispered back. It was the first week of December.

Barry dug his index finger and thumb into my shoulder muscle. "Ten minutes, or die."

"Okay!" I jerked my shoulder away.

Barry turned and went out through the cafeteria doors. Everyone at our table stayed quiet for a moment. Josh pursed his lips. Amber looked away, as if trying to spare me any more embarrassment than necessary.

Alex gave me a commiserating look. "It's been nice knowing you, Jake."

4

Four and a half minutes later I dropped my un-eaten baked potato into the garbage. After that "visit" from Barry, I'd lost my appetite.

"Want us to come with you?" Andy asked as we dumped our lunch trays.

I shook my head. "It'll just get him mad."

"If you're not back in five minutes, I'm telling Mr. Braun," Josh said.

Five minutes with Barry Dunn was an eternity. If he felt like it, he could do a lot of damage in that much time. I left my friends and went out through the cafeteria doors. Outside it was a cold, dreary day. The grass was covered by a thin film of frozen dew, and the sky was a solid blanket of gray. It felt like it was going to snow. Wearing only a long-sleeve shirt, I shivered and watched my breath turn to white vapor.

The garage at the Burt Itchupt Middle School (we called it Burp It Up) was a low gray building on the other side of the bus circle. Dirtbags like

Barry and his buddies went back there to smoke cigarettes and torture kids like me. Crossing the bus circle alone, I felt like I was walking down death row.

Barry and a couple of his friends were waiting back there. One of his friends was wearing a black football jacket, the other a gray sweat shirt. Barry was wearing a T-shirt. His bare arms had turned red in the cold, but he had to show everyone how tough he was.

The first thing he did was blow an air hanky, alternately holding one nostril closed while snorting out the other. I'd never seen him do that before. It must have been a newly acquired skill.

He wiped his nose with his bare arm to clean up any nasal residue, then slid his right foot forward. The laces of his untied shoe hung down in the dirt. "Tie it."

I stared down at his shoe. Barry loved inflicting humiliation as much as he did pain. From deep inside I mustered just enough courage to say, "Tie it yourself."

Barry squinted at me. "I didn't hear you good."

"Well, that's not quite right," I said, desperately trying to stall. "Actually, you didn't hear me *correctly*."

"Huh?" Barry's forehead wrinkled. He wasn't the smartest kid in the world. In fact, some kids called him "The Dunce" behind his back.

"'I didn't hear you good' is bad English," I explained.

"I don't care what language it is." Barry made a fist. "Tie or die."

The situation looked bad. If I didn't think of something fast I would have to choose between severe humiliation or a severe beating.

"You know what worries me?" I asked.

"Now what?" Barry snapped impatiently.

"Making me tie your shoes sort of implies that you never learned to tie them yourself."

Barry frowned. "Get off it."

I turned to his dirtbag buddies. "Every time you see him, his laces are untied, right?"

They nodded. Barry never tied his shoes. The laces were always flapping loosely on the ground. Barry turned to his friends, who were now giving him funny looks.

"Oh, come on," he sputtered. "You know I can."

His friends didn't look convinced. So Barry kneeled down and tied his own shoe. Then he looked up at us. "See?"

"Knew you could do it." I gave Barry a wink and started back toward the cafeteria.

5

I made it halfway across the bus circle before Barry and his friends caught up to me. Barry's face had turned red, but it looked like it was more from anger than the cold.

"You think you're smart, Sherman," he growled, making a fist. "Now you're really gonna pay."

If the situation had looked bad before, it really looked bleak now. Barry and his friends were blocking my path back to the cafeteria. I realized I'd made a major tactical error. By making Barry look dumb in front of his friends, I'd made him *really* mad. Mad enough to start a fight right there in the bus circle where everyone in the cafeteria could watch.

But instead of throwing a punch, Barry slid his left shoe forward. "Tie it."

I looked down at the shoe. The situation had just gone from bleak to bleakest. This was a hundred times worse than before. If I tied Barry's shoe now, the whole cafeteria would see.

"Tie or die." Barry glowered.

My heart had started to pound, and I looked around quickly for a way out of this.

"If I refuse and you beat me up, everyone'll see," I said, trying to buy time. "You'll get sent to the office. Principal Blanco will definitely suspend you."

"Good," Barry grumbled. "I could use some time off from this crummy place. Now *tie it*."

I felt a sick sensation in my stomach. By now everyone in the cafeteria was probably looking out the windows. Josh was probably taking bets on how much blood I was about to lose.

"Quit stalling." Barry made a fist and held it in front of my nose.

Just then the cafeteria door swung open and Mr. Braun came out. Barry and his friends didn't see him because they had their backs to the cafeteria. In the following nanosecond I went from abject terror to total relief.

"You know, Barry," I said. "I really think you should reconsider."

Barry made a face as if he'd just sucked on something really sour. "What?"

"I'd really hate to have to kick your brains in," I said. "Of course, that's provided I can *find* your brains. I know they can't be in your head. I guess I'd have to start with your toes and work my way up."

Barry's eyes bulged out of his head. He gnashed his teeth and pulled back his fist to deliver a major bone-crushing punch to my face.

Slap! A hand clamped on Barry's arm, stopping him from throwing the punch.

Barry spun around and came face to face with Mr. Braun.

"Chill out, Dunn. No fighting," the gym teacher warned.

Barry quickly pointed at me. "But he . . ." His voice trailed off.

"He what?" Mr. Braun crossed his massive arms and waited.

Barry's eyes shot laser beams of fury at me. He couldn't tell Mr. Braun that I'd made fun of the size of his brain, and that was why he was about to massacre me.

"Move it, Dunn." Mr. Braun pointed back toward the cafeteria, then nodded at Barry's friends. "You, too. I see any of you lay a finger on Sherman, you'll be cleaning the shower room with a toothbrush."

"You're dead meat, Jake," Barry grumbled, and headed back to the cafeteria.

6

My teeth had started to chatter in the cold, but I chose to wait until Barry and his friends went back into the cafeteria. Maybe I'd even wait until the next period before I went back inside. Barry Dunn was just enough of a head case to hang around inside the doors and pound me when I came in.

"What's the problem, Sherman?" Mr. Braun asked. He was standing in the middle of the bus circle with his arms crossed. He didn't look cold at all. Maybe all those muscles worked like insulation. I shoved my hands in my pockets and shivered. I wasn't going to tell him anything.

"Let me give you a word of advice," Mr. Braun said. "The only way to stop Barry Dunn is to stand up to him."

That caught me by surprise. "You mean, fight back? But we're not supposed to do that."

"Who says?" Mr. Braun asked.

"Principal Blanco, the teachers, everyone."

"Principal Blanco can't tell kids to hit back,"

15

Mr. Braun said. "There'd be a hundred fights a day. But *I'm* telling you, nobody admires a wuss. And you'll never get a good girlfriend either. You think Bertha would have anything to do with me if I was a wuss?"

Bertha was Mr. Braun's girlfriend. He talked about her all the time.

"But we're supposed find other ways to settle our differences," I said. "That's what they've been teaching us since kindergarten. We're supposed to develop coping mechanisms and act *mature*."

Mr. Braun shook his head. "Don't give me that psychological mumbo jumbo. It's time to start acting like a man, Sherman. Not a yellow-bellied *wuss*."

I glared back at him. I was really tired of hearing him call me a wuss.

7

"Can I ask what you are *doing*, Jake?" Andy said. He, Josh, and I were in my room after school, watching *Total Recall*, the movie where Arnold Schwarzenegger blows away about 100 bad guys a minute. We hung out in my room a lot after school because I had a 27-inch TV and VCR, lots of junk food and, best of all, my parents were never around.

At that moment I was on my stomach under my bed. "Braun said it was time for me to act like a man."

"Then why are you crawling around under your bed like a cockroach?" Josh asked.

"To find this." I shoved a barbell and some weights out. Lance, my yellow Labrador retriever, came over and sniffed them curiously. Then he lay down at the end of the bed and went back to sleep.

Across the room, Josh was sitting with his feet up on my desk. His arm disappeared into a family-size bag of chips. A two liter bottle of Coke stood on the floor beside him. Josh had reddish hair, freckles, and a lot of extra beef around his waist.

"What are you gonna do with those?" He pulled a large, perfect potato chip out of the bag and popped it into his mouth.

"He's gonna plant them in the backyard and see if they'll grow muscles," Andy cracked.

"I just want to try it." I slid a couple of weights on the bar, then reached down and hoisted it up to my chest.

"You're really gonna start lifting weights?" Josh asked uneasily.

"Maybe." I grunted and pushed the bar over my head.

Andy reached into the bag of chips, felt around for a good one, and pulled it out. "You heard Mr. Braun today. It'll take you *at least* fifteen years to get muscles like his. And that's lifting *every day*."

"You gotta start somewhere." Huffing and puffing, I lowered the bar back to my chest, then pressed it up again.

"I know why he's doing it," Josh teased. "He wants to get a world-class girlfriend like Bertha."

"I thought he was in love with Amber," Andy said.

"Shut up," I grumbled.

"Or what? You're gonna beat me up with your

brand-new muscles?" Andy grinned.

"I'd take Bertha over Amber any day," Josh said.

"Why?" Andy asked. "No one's ever seen her. Braun just *talks* about her."

"He's got a picture of her in the gym office," Josh said. "I saw it today. She's a real babe. And you know where she is right now?"

"In Jake's closet?" Andy guessed and then pretended to be a TV announcer. *"And now, ladies and gentlemen, the surprise you've all been waiting for! In Jake Sherman's closet . . . it's Bertha the babe!"*

"She's at the Ms. Galaxy Pageant, snotwad," Josh said.

"Never heard of it," Andy replied.

"Ever hear of the Miss America Pageant?" Josh asked. "Or the Miss Universe Pageant? It's a beauty contest, dimwit."

In the movie, Arnold was mowing down bad guys left and right. I pressed the barbell again. If I was going to stand up to Dunn "The Dunce" and "be a man," I would have to get a lot stronger first.

Josh pulled another potato chip out of the bag. "You trying to build strength or big muscles?"

"Isn't it all the same?" I grimaced as I pressed the bar up for a fourth time.

Josh shook his head. "You get strength by doing a lot of reps with medium weight. Big muscles

19

you get by lifting really heavy weight just a few times."

"When did you become such an expert?" Andy asked, grabbing the bag and pulling out a chip.

"Read it in *Sports Illustrated*," Josh answered.

I put the bar down on the floor and added more weight to it.

"Whoa, looks like Jake's going for the big muscles," Andy said with a chuckle.

"I just want to try it." But before picking up the bar again, I stuck my hand in the bag, pulled out a bunch of broken chiplets, and stuffed them in my mouth.

Josh yanked the bag away. "Can't you ever take one chip at a time like a normal person?"

"Bug off." I closed my hands around the bar and pulled up. With the extra weight it was super heavy. I managed to straighten up, but couldn't get the bar higher than my waist.

"You have to squat down really fast and yank it up under your chin," Josh said.

"You read that in *Sports Illustrated*, too?" Andy asked.

"Saw it on TV," Josh said. "It's called the clean and jerk."

"*You're* the clean and jerk," Andy quipped.

"And you're the *dirt* and jerk," Josh shot back.

I squatted down and yanked. *CRUNK!* The barbell slipped out of my grip and crashed to the floor.

Owwoooooo! Lance jumped to his feet and let out a startled howl.

"Nice going, Jake." Josh grinned.

"I'd like to see *you* do better, Mr. Flabola." I picked up the bag of chips and pulled out another handful.

Josh grabbed the bag away. "One at a time!" Then he swung his feet off the desk, squatted down behind the bar, and closed his hands around it.

"Uhhhhhhh!" He let out a long groan and managed to get the bar about three inches off the floor before letting it go with a *thunk!*

"Forget it." Breathing hard, Josh slumped back into the chair and took a swig of Coke.

Now Andy got behind the bar and grabbed it. "Hey, no fair! It's covered with potato chip grease. You can't get a grip."

"Good excuse." Josh smirked.

Andy grabbed the bar anyway, and managed to get it up to his waist, but couldn't get it any higher.

He'd just put the bar down when the door opened and my sister Jessica stuck her head in. Jessica had thick brown hair, which she wore in a braid down her back. She was in tenth grade, a major brain pain, and a jock. This year she was seriously into soccer, basketball, and lacrosse.

"Where's the earthquake?" she asked.

"Josh burped," Andy said.

21

"Get stuffed," Josh grumbled.

"Uh-oh, the human trash compactor is peeved," Andy said.

Josh shook his fist at him.

"I dropped the weights." I pointed at the barbell on the floor.

"Ow, wow, don't tell me the Couch Potato Club has decided to do something semi-athletic." Jessica squatted down behind the bar. I smiled at Josh and Andy. Josh winked back. A couple of days a week my sister worked out at the Burn Center, a health club in town, but there was *no way* she was going to get that bar off the floor.

In a series of quick movements, Jessica yanked the bar to her waist, squatted and got it up to her chin, then pressed it until her arms were extended and the bar was high over her head. Then she quickly put the bar down.

"Piece of cake, but you should wipe off the potato chip grease." She dusted her hands and left.

Andy and I shared a dismal look.

"Show-off," Josh muttered.

I reached for the bag and took a handful of chiplets.

"One at a time!" Josh growled.

Without another word, we sat down and watched Arnold slaughter a few hundred bad guys.

8

The next day I walked down the hall at school with Amber. It was the last period and we were headed for the gym.

"So what do you call someone who lies near the front door all day?" I asked.

"I don't know," she said.

"Matt," I said.

Amber smiled. That always made me feel good.

"What about someone who hangs on the wall?" I asked.

"Uh . . . Spider?" she guessed.

"Art."

The lines in Amber's forehead creased for a moment. "Hangs on the wall? Oh, I get it!"

"How about — "

"Getting out of my way," Barry Dunn growled before I could finish the next joke. He was standing in the middle of the hall, blocking our path.

"Think you're smart, don't you?" Barry snarled.

"I get by," I said.

"Try getting by *this!*" Barry stomped down as hard as he could on my foot with the heel of his shoe. A bolt of throbbing pain radiated up my leg and I had to grit my teeth to keep from crying out.

Barry gave me a nasty grin. "Next time it'll be worse." Then he marched away toward the gym.

I had to limp the rest of the way down the hall. It felt like he'd crushed a couple of toes.

"Does it hurt?" Amber asked.

I gave her a look.

"Sorry, dumb question," she apologized. "Barry's such a jerk. I wish there was something you could do about him."

I winced. I'm sure Amber didn't mean to add insult to injury, but basically she was implying that I couldn't beat him up by myself so I'd have to find some other way to deal with him. In other words, I was a wuss.

We got to the gym, which was filled with dozens of plywood tables.

"What's going on?" I asked.

"They're setting up for the science fair tomorrow," Amber said. "Guess we'll be running relay races in the halls today."

The girls' locker room was on the other side of the gym, so Amber headed in that direction. I limped into the boys' locker room.

Just outside the locker room doors was the gym office. Through the window I could see Mr. Braun

24

sitting at his desk, squeezing a red rubber ball in his hand. I knocked.

The gym teacher looked up and saw me in the window. "Door's open, Sherman."

I went in. Mr. Braun kept squeezing the red ball. He noticed that I was watching.

"Hand strength, Sherman," he explained. "When you're dead lifting five hundred pounds, you need it."

"I'll keep than in mind, Mr. Braun," I said. "Meanwhile, can I be excused from gym today?"

"Got a note?" he asked.

"It just happened," I said.

"What just happened?"

"Someone stomped on my foot." Just at that very second, Barry Dunn walked past the office window.

"I see," Mr. Braun said, gazing out the window. "Sorry, Sherman. No note, no gloat."

"But I can hardly walk," I said.

"Don't worry," Mr. Braun said. "I'll find something for you to do."

9

"What happened to you?" Alex watched me limp down a row of gym lockers and sit on the bench near him. His locker was just a few feet from mine.

"Dunn crushed my foot." I whispered because Barry also had gym that period, and his locker was one row over.

Alex's eyes darted around. "He here yet?"

"Yeah, I just saw him. Why?"

Instead of answering, Alex reached into his pocket and took out a short, fat metal spring. "Stole this from tech shop. As soon as Dunn leaves his locker, put this in his lock."

Alex got up and went around the corner. A moment later a voice that sounded just like Mr. Braun's bellowed, "Dunn, in my office, now!"

"Aw, man, now what?" A row over, Barry groaned and headed for Mr. Braun's office. I quietly slipped into his row. He'd been in the middle of changing into his gym clothes, and had left his locker open. I dropped the spring in the lock, then hurried back to my locker.

A few seconds later Barry returned. A moment after that, Alex sat down next to me on the bench.

"You do it?" he whispered.

"Yeah."

"Great. Take your time changing. We have to let The Dunce leave first."

It wasn't long before we heard a locker slam shut and Barry passed again, this time wearing shorts, a T-shirt, and sneakers with untied laces.

"Come on!" Alex whispered. We slipped around the corner and into the row with Barry's locker. The locker room was almost empty now. The spring had stopped Barry's lock from closing completely. Alex opened the locker and gazed in.

"Perfect!" He grabbed Barry's shoes.

We ran down to the toilet stalls. Inside one, Alex unlaced the shoes halfway, and slid the laces around the hinge that held the toilet seat to the toilet. Then he started tying knots.

"Tie lots of them." He gestured for me to do the other shoe. "And make sure they're really *tight!*"

10

"Where's my shoes?" Barry growled at the end of the gym.

Sitting in front of our lockers one aisle over, Alex and I winked at each other and changed out of our gym clothes. You had three choices when stuff disappeared from your gym locker. You could search through the dozens of empty lockers scattered around the locker room. You could look outside. Or you could look in the bathroom. Kids usually checked the bathroom first, since that was the easiest.

Barry headed for the bathroom. A moment later we heard him scream, *"Someone's gonna die for this!"*

All around the locker room kids smiled. While it was true that Barry picked on me more than anyone else, he wasn't all that choosy. At one time or another, he'd hurt most of the guys in our class. So almost everyone was pleased to see him get it back.

Alex and I finished changing. As we strolled out of the locker room, we casually glanced through the open stall door where Barry was bent over a toilet, grumbling furiously as he tried to undo all the knots in his shoelaces.

"Ahem!" We were just about to leave the gym when someone cleared his throat behind us. Alex and I turned and saw Mr. Braun standing in the doorway of the gym office with his arms crossed.

"Let's talk, boys." He gestured for Alex and me to enter his office. We gave each other an apprehensive look.

"Busted," Alex mumbled under his breath.

11

"Sneaking around like that isn't going to solve your problems." Mr. Braun was sitting behind his dark green metal desk. Alex and I were sitting in two old wooden chairs across from him. The desk was covered with papers, a phone, and a photograph of a really pretty blond woman. I assumed she was Bertha, Mr. Braun's girlfriend. The photo only showed her face, but I could see why she was a contestant for the Ms. Galaxy Pageant. Like Josh had said, she was really pretty.

"All you're doing is making Dunn madder," Mr. Braun went on. "And the madder he gets, the more he's going to pick on people. And since he doesn't know who tied his shoes to the toilet, he's going to pick on everyone."

"How do *you* know who did it?" Alex asked.

"A little birdy told me," Mr. Braun said. Alex and I shared a defeated look. There were a couple of teacher's pets in the class who could always be counted on to squeal.

"So what are you gonna do to us?" Alex asked.

"The question is, what are *you* going to do about Barry Dunn?" Mr. Braun replied. "Until one of you little runts stands up to him, he's going to keep picking on everyone."

"Barry would kill us," Alex said. "Why don't *you* stand up to him?"

"That's not my job, Silver, it's yours."

"Well, most of the time we manage to fake him out," I said. "Maybe we don't have big muscles, but Barry's not too big in the brain department. It kind of balances out."

"Or maybe you've just been lucky," Mr. Braun said. "Brains will get you just so far, Sherman. One of these days it's gonna come down to *mano a mano*. Your fists will have to do the talking. You'll have to act like a man."

Buzzzzzzz! Outside the bell rang. Alex sighed and shook his head hopelessly. The idea of trying to fight Barry Dunn was ridiculous. He was the biggest, strongest kid at Burp It Up Middle School.

"Well, thanks for the advice, Mr. Braun," Alex said, a little sarcastically as he rose from his chair. "School's over. Can we go or is this, like, detention?"

Rap! Rap! Before Mr. Braun could answer, someone knocked on the gym office door. The door swung open and Mr. Dirksen, the science teacher, stuck his head in.

31

"What can I do for you, Phil?" Mr. Braun asked.

"I have to move something heavy into the gym for the science fair," Mr. Dirksen said, looking more at Alex and me than at Mr. Braun. "And I was hoping to find a few strong backs."

Mr. Braun smiled at Alex. "Looks like the answer to your question is yes, Silver, this is detention. And while you're here, you can help Mr. Dirksen move his stuff. Go get your coats, boys. It's snowing outside."

12

Alex and I got our coats and followed Mr. Dirksen out to the parking lot. It had started to snow really hard. The white stuff was coming down so fast that we couldn't even see the far end of the parking lot.

"So, Jake, having a good year?" Mr. Dirksen asked as we trekked through the snow.

"Not really," I said.

"Why not?" he asked.

"Barry Dunn's a major pain."

Mr. Dirksen nodded. He and I had accidentally switched bodies in sixth grade. After that I'd tried to behave better in school. Mr. Dirksen had gotten a toupee and tried to be less boring. He'd improved, but the old saying still applied: "Once a dweeb, always a dweeb."

We stopped next to a yellow rented van and Mr. Dirksen opened the back doors. Inside was some familiar-looking science equipment.

"It's the experiment!" I said. "You finally got it to work?"

Mr. Dirksen's experiment was supposed to transfer intelligence from one creature to another, but it accidentally switched people's bodies instead. Not only had I gotten stuck in Mr. Dirksen's body, but Andy had once switched bodies with my dog, Lance.

"I believe I have, Jake," said Mr. Dirksen. "At the science fair tomorrow, I hope to show that I can transfer trained behavior from one mouse to another."

Alex had taken a computer monitor out of the van and was trudging through the snow back to the gym. I stepped closer to Mr. Dirksen.

"So you've fixed it so it won't make people switch bodies anymore?" I asked in a low voice.

"Absolutely, Jake," Mr. Dirksen assured me. "That will *never* happen again."

13

It wasn't long before we carried all of the equipment into the gym and started to set it up. The experiment was so big that we had to push two plywood tables together. We were in the middle of assembling everything when Principal Blanco came in. He was a former gym teacher, a short, pudgy man with short curly black hair. He was wearing a green parka with a fur-lined hood.

"Afterschool activities are cancelled," he announced. "The snow's knocking down power lines all over the place. Some of us have long trips home and we're not going to make it if we wait much longer. How are you boys going to get home?"

"I'll call my mom," Alex said. "We've got four-wheel drive."

Alex went out to the pay phone in the hall. Principal Blanco turned to Mr. Dirksen. "What about you, Phil?"

"I guess I'll head home now," Mr. Dirksen said.

Mr. Braun came out of the gym office. "Why

don't you go home, too," he said to Principal Blanco. "I only live a few blocks away. I'll wait here until the boys get picked up."

"Thanks, Teddy, I appreciate it," Principal Blanco said. "Make sure you lock up tight."

I'd never heard anyone call Mr. Braun by his first name before. *Teddy?* Talk about a wuss name.

Pretty soon, the only people left in the gym were Alex, Mr. Braun, and me. Having nothing better to do, I kept assembling Mr. Dirksen's experiment. I'd assembled it with him once before and pretty much knew where everything went. It was kind of fun, like putting together a big model.

"Oh, man!" Alex suddenly groaned. "I didn't tell my mom which entrance to use. She's gonna go to the main entrance instead of the gym."

"Can you call her?" Mr. Braun asked.

"Naw, she's probably left by now." Alex pulled on his coat. "I'll have to go outside and flag her down."

Alex went outside, leaving Mr. Braun and me alone in the gym. It was really quiet.

"This is some contraption," Mr. Braun said, looking over Mr. Dirksen's experiment. "How do you know where everything goes?"

I told him how I'd helped Mr. Dirksen put it together once before. Mr. Braun wanted to know what it did and how it worked, so I explained it as best as I could. And explained it again, and again, because he didn't catch on too quickly. Meanwhile I plugged the heavy black electrical cables into the wall sockets. I wanted to make sure I'd connected everything correctly. Lights came on and the machine began to hum.

"Wow," said Mr. Braun.

Phoom! Suddenly the lights went out and Mr. Dirksen's experiment stopped humming. The gym went totally black. It was a weird sensation. Almost like you didn't know which way was up.

"Sherman?" Mr. Braun asked. It was so dark that I couldn't see him. I couldn't even see my hand in front of my face.

"Yeah?"

"A power line must've come down," he said. "Don't worry. The school put in a new emergency generator over the summer. It should kick in any second."

Whuuummmmpp! The next thing I knew, an explosion knocked me off my feet.

14

"What happened?" a voice asked in the dark. It sounded too young to be Mr. Braun's.

"Who said that?" I was groggy and dizzy, and wondered if I'd been unconscious for a few moments. The air smelled funny, and my voice sounded strange. Much deeper than usual. Maybe my ears had been messed up by the explosion.

"I did," the voice said.

"Who are you?" I asked.

"Mr. Braun, who else?"

Still in a daze, I pushed myself up to my feet. For some strange reason my clothes felt tight. I wished I could see, but everything was pitch-black.

"Something must've gone wrong with the emergency generator," Mr. Braun said. "You okay?"

"I guess." But I wasn't okay. Something was definitely weird. Not only did the clothes I was wearing feel tight, but my hair felt different. I ran my hand over my jaw.

I had stubble!

"Sherman?" Mr. Braun's voice had a tinge of uncertainty . . . as if he'd just felt *his* jaw. "I think something strange is going on."

In the dark I felt my arms. They were huge and bulging. My stomach was as hard as a washboard. My neck felt like a tree trunk.

There was only one explanation.

It had happened again!

15

Meanwhile, Mr. Braun was talking to himself in the dark. "These aren't my clothes. There has to be a light somewhere. I need a mirror. Something crazy's going on. What happened to my voice?"

Down at the other end of the gym, a door creaked open. "Jake? Mr. Braun?" Alex called into the dark. "You guys okay?"

"Yeah," I called back. "Your mom here?"

"Not yet, Mr. Braun," Alex replied. "But all the lights went out. I heard an explosion. I came in to make sure everything was all right."

"Everything's fine," I said. "Go wait for your mom. We'll be out in a second."

The door creaked shut. The gym was still pitch-black.

"What's going on, Sherman?" Mr. Braun's, I mean, my voice quavered.

"You better call me Mr. Braun," I said. We'd switched bodies. The funny thing was, the more I thought about it, the more I *liked* it.

"What are you talking about?" he asked. "You're not me. I am."

"Not anymore."

The door at the end of the gym creaked again. "Guys?" Alex called. "She's here."

"Come on, we better go," I said.

"Go where?" Mr. Braun, I mean, I asked in the dark. "I'm not going with you. I'm going home."

"You're not old enough to drive," I said.

"Get off it, Sherman."

"I told you to call me Mr. Braun."

"Hey, you guys coming or what?" Alex called from the other side of the gym.

"I don't know what this is about, Sherman, but I've had enough of this game. Unless you want to clean the bathroom with a toothbrush for the rest of the year, you better tell me what's going on."

"You wouldn't believe me." I started to feel my way around the plywood tables in the dark. Every time I bumped into one, it made a squeak as its legs scraped on the gym floor.

"Hey, where are you going?" Mr. Braun, in my body, called behind me.

"Out of the gym. I'm not spending the night here."

"But I can't find my keys."

I reached into my, I mean, Mr. Braun's pocket and pulled out a heavy ring of keys, then jingled them in the dark. "They're right here."

"Give 'em to me."

"No way, Sherman."

"Don't call me Sherman!" Mr. Braun snarled. *Screeeck!* "Ow!" He must've banged into a table.

"Careful, Sherman," I said. "That's my body you're banging around."

"*Stop calling me Sherman!*" he shouted. "I'm Braun. And when I get you, you're gonna be sorry."

"What's with you guys?" Alex called from the other end of the gym.

"Sherman's just a little freaked," I said.

"*I am not!*" he shouted. *Screeeck!* He banged into another table. "Ow!"

"Take it easy, Sherman," I said.

"You're gonna pay for this!" *Screeeck!* "Ow!"

"Hey, Jake, chill," Alex said.

"*Don't call me —* "

Phoom! Suddenly the lights went back on.

I had to squint in the brightness, but as my eyes adjusted, I looked down at myself. I was wearing Mr. Braun's sweatpants and dark blue polo shirt. I had his massive arms, legs, and hands. Several tables away, Mr. Braun was looking down at himself, I mean, myself. He pulled my shirt away from my body. He stared at my hands, then squeezed my arms. With my fingers he felt my face. Then, with an expression of total disbelief and astonishment, he looked across the gym at me, I mean, himself.

"No! I don't believe it!" he gasped.

"Don't believe what?" Alex asked from the doorway.

"Sherman and I switched bodies!" Mr. Braun cried.

"What?" Alex looked at him like he was crazy.

"Sherman bumped his head," I said. "I think he's a little confused."

Mr. Braun's jaw dropped and his eyes widened. "Why you!" In my body, he charged between the tables at me.

16

He tried to hit me, but I grabbed him by the shirt collar and held him back. He started hitting my arm, but it didn't hurt much. It was kind of depressing. I'd never realized what a weakling I was.

"Chill out, Jake," Alex warned. "You can't hit Mr. Braun. You want to get suspended?"

He stopped swinging and glared at Alex. "I'm telling you for the last time! I'm not Jake! I'm Ted Braun!"

Alex frowned and glanced quizzically at me.

"Head trauma," I said.

Alex nodded gravely. "Come on, Jake, my mom's waiting. We gotta go."

"I have to come with you," I said.

The lines in Alex's forehead deepened. "Why, Mr. Braun?"

"My car doesn't have snow tires," I said. "I'll never make it home."

"Well, okay, I guess we can drop you off at your place," Alex said.

That was a problem. I didn't know where Mr. Braun lived, and I really didn't want to go there anyway.

"I better go home with Jake and make sure he's okay," I said.

Alex gave me a puzzled look, then looked at Jake, who in turn was staring at me.

"You really want me to stay in your apartment tonight?" I whispered to him.

Jake, I mean, Mr. Braun, blinked as if he hadn't thought about that. I couldn't blame him. I'd been through this once before, but Mr. Braun had never been in someone else's body.

Finally he shook his head. "No."

17

A little while later, Mrs. Silver turned her Jeep down Magnolia Street. It was dark and all we could see were millions of flakes in the car's headlights. On the radio we'd heard that the storm would probably continue through the night.

"Bet we'll have a snow day tomorrow," Alex said happily from the front seat. "You want to shovel driveways?"

It was clear that he was addressing Jake, but Mr. Braun, in my body, was gazing out the window, not paying attention. I gave him a nudge with my, I mean, his elbow.

"Huh?" he turned.

"Silver asked if you want to shovel driveways tomorrow."

Jake frowned. It looked like he was going to say no.

"Maybe you'll want to talk in the morning," I suggested.

"Okay." Alex nodded.

Mrs. Silver pulled up in front of my house. I reached for the door. "Thanks for the ride, Mrs. Silver."

"You're welcome, Mr. Braun," Alex's mother replied.

Jake, I mean, Mr. Braun, and I got out of the car and started up the walk. The drifts were deep and difficult to walk through. Blowing snow stung our faces.

"Wait a minute." Jake, I mean, Mr. Braun stopped behind me.

"What?" I asked.

"I'm going back to school," he said.

Now he really *was* acting crazy. "Why?"

"If that machine switched us, it can switch us back."

"Not without me it can't," I said.

Mr. Braun stood in the snow wearing my clothes and staring at me with my eyes. "Don't you want to switch back?"

"I don't know," I said.

"What do you mean?" he gasped. "You can't just keep my body."

"Who says?" I asked.

"I do."

I smiled. "Chill out, *Sherman*." I started through the snow toward the front door again, but a few steps later I stopped. Mr. Braun was standing in the middle of a drift with a stunned look on my face.

"You say anything to my parents or sister about this and you'll *never* get your body back, understand?" I warned him. "You saw what happened with Alex. No one'll believe you anyway."

"But it's true," he insisted. "They'll *have* to believe me."

"Oh, sure." I grinned. "Like people switch bodies every day."

The funny thing was that my sister *would* have believed him because she'd seen it happen before. But Mr. Braun didn't know that. As far as he knew, it had never happened before.

I pushed open the front door and stamped my feet on the inside mat. Mr. Braun, in my body, followed me in.

"That you, Jake?" Jessica called from her room upstairs.

I had to give Jake another nudge. "Answer her," I whispered.

"Uh, yeah, it's me," Mr. Braun, in my body, called up the stairs.

"I left some lasagna for you in the kitchen," Jessica yelled. "Mom and Dad called from the city. They didn't think they could get home in this weather so they're staying at a hotel tonight. Make sure you feed Lance and let him out."

I gave Mr. Braun, in my body, a meaningful look.

"Uh, sure," he called up the stairs.

My, I mean, Mr. Braun's stomach was growling. "You hungry?" I asked.

"I guess."

"Well, I'm starved," I said. "Come on."

I headed for the kitchen and stepped over Lance's wooden gate. Lance was usually allowed everywhere in the house, but on the nights when my parents weren't around, we put the burglar alarm on and kept him in the kitchen so he wouldn't set it off accidentally.

Grrrrrrrrr! On the other side of the kitchen, Lance stood up and growled when he saw me. The hair on his back rose and his tail dropped. He bared his teeth . . . and attacked!

18

"No! Lance, it's me!" I shouted. "Stop!"

Lance didn't seem to hear. At the last second I jumped back over the gate.

Grrrroooof! Lance skidded into the gate and barked angrily.

"Hey, come on." I kneeled down and got eye to eye with him. "That's no way to treat an old friend, is it?"

Grrrrrrrrrr! Lance still growled, but with less certainty than before. I pressed my, I mean, Mr. Braun's hand against the gate. Lance sniffed it warily.

"You better let me come in," I said. "Otherwise I can't give you dinner."

Arf! At the word "dinner" Lance started to smile and wag his tail. I stood up, winked at Mr. Braun in my body, and stepped over the gate again.

I gave Lance dinner, but when I opened the kitchen door to let him out into the backyard, he took one look at all that snow and backed away.

"Can't say I blame you," I said, closing the kitchen door. Lance went back to his dog bed and lay down. I went over to the kitchen counter where half of a microwaved lasagna dinner was covered with foil. That wasn't enough for me to eat, much less for me and Mr. Braun, I mean, Jake. That's when I noticed that he wasn't in the kitchen.

"Jake?" I walked back to the gate. Jake, I mean, Mr. Braun, was standing on the other side.

"Want something to eat?" I asked.

Jake, I mean, Mr. Braun nodded.

"Then come on in." I gestured for him to step over the gate.

Mr. Braun hesitated. "Where is he?"

"Who?"

"The dog."

"Lance? In here. Why?"

Mr. Braun, in my body, didn't answer. He didn't come into the kitchen either.

"He won't hurt you," I said.

"How do *you* know?"

"Because he didn't hurt me and he doesn't even *know* me," I said. "He's known *you* all his life."

"But I don't know him," Mr. Braun said.

"Yes, you do," I said. "You've known him since he was a puppy."

Mr. Braun, in my body, scowled. "I've never seen him before."

I sighed. "You've known him since he was a puppy because you're me, remember?"

Mr. Braun still didn't budge.

"Now what's the problem?" I asked.

"I, uh, don't like dogs."

"How can you not like dogs?" I asked.

"Well, I've just never . . ." He didn't finish. Lance had gotten up to see who I was talking to. Mr. Braun, in my body, backed away.

"You mean, you're *scared* of him?" I had to smile.

Mr. Braun grit my teeth.

"I don't believe it!" I laughed. "The great and mighty Mr. Braun is scared of *a dog*? What are you, *a wuss*?"

Mr. Braun clenched my fists and bristled.

I pointed a muscular finger at him. "Hey, I'd watch it if I were you. Don't forget what happened before in the gym."

"Maybe you'd like to tell *me* what happened," someone said.

19

I looked up, surprised. Jessica was standing at the other end of the hall.

"Who are you, anyway?" she asked warily. "You look familiar."

"I'm, uh, the new physical education teacher at the middle school," I said.

"Why do I feel like I know you?" Jessica asked.

I glanced nervously at Mr. Braun, in my body, but he shook his head as if he didn't know either.

"What are you doing here?" my sister asked.

"Well, uh, because of the snowstorm I didn't think I could make it all the way home," I said. "Sherman . . . I mean, Jake, was nice enough to invite me to stay here tonight."

"Don't you think you should have asked Mom and Dad first?" Jessica directed the question at Jake.

"I guess." Mr. Braun, in my body, answered with a believable shrug.

Jessica turned back to me. "I'm not trying to be rude, Mr. . . ."

"Braun," I said.

"Mr. Braun, I'm not trying to be rude," Jessica said. "But our parents aren't here and Jake knows he's supposed to ask for permission before he does something like this."

"I won't be any bother," I said. "And I plan to leave first thing in the morning. By then the roads will be plowed. I'll walk back to school, dig out my car, and go home."

Jessica didn't look happy. She glanced at Jake. "Where's he going to sleep?"

"Uh . . ." Jake's eyes darted toward me.

"The guest room in the basement," I said.

"How'd you know about that?" Jessica scowled.

"Jake told me about it on the way here."

"Well, I guess it's all right." Jessica still didn't look happy. "Just don't leave me a big mess in the kitchen, okay, Jake?"

Jessica was always bugging me about leaving the kitchen neat.

"Come with me, Lance." She clapped her hands. Lance got up and followed her back upstairs. I was glad because I was *starving*. I guess it took a lot of food to feed a body like Mr. Braun's. That half-finished lasagna was starting to look mighty tempting.

"You want any of this?" I gestured to the lasagna as Mr. Braun, in my body, came into the kitchen.

"Okay." He nodded my head. I'd kind of been hoping he'd say no so I could eat the whole thing myself. But being a courteous host, I chopped it in half with a knife, slid my half on a plate, and ate it in three bites. Then I started rooting around the kitchen for more to eat. I made a triple-decker peanut butter and jelly sandwich, and followed it up with a box of strawberry Pop-Tarts, a bowl of Frosted Flakes, and a bag of chips. I washed it all down with a liter of Coke.

Meanwhile, Jake, I mean, Mr. Braun went through the refrigerator and took out stuff for a salad. For dinner he had the remaining lasagna, salad, bread *without* butter, and a bowl of canned pineapple for dessert.

Mr. Braun was real quiet while we ate. He looked almost like he was . . . *thinking.*

"Want some chips?" I asked, holding the bag out toward him.

He shook his head. "You eat like this all the time?"

"Sure," I said. "Only usually I don't eat as much."

"Do you have any idea how much cholesterol, saturated fat, sodium, sugar, and *preservatives* you've just consumed?" he asked.

I shrugged. "Didn't really think about it."

"You have to stop eating this way," he said.

"I don't have to do *anything.*" I grabbed another handful of chips and stuffed them into my, I mean, Mr. Braun's mouth.

He sighed wearily. "Listen, maybe you don't care what you do to your *own* body, but you could be a little more considerate about how you treat mine."

"Looks who's talking," I said. "*You're* the one that went around smashing my body into those tables in the gym."

"It's *who*," Mr. Braun said.

"What's who?" I asked.

" 'You're the one *who* went around smashing into tables,' " he said. "Not '*that* went around.' "

I stared at him in disbelief. "You're correcting *my* English? You're just a *kid*."

"No, I'm a physical education teacher stuck in a kid's body," he replied.

"Whatever," I grumbled. "Either way, don't tell me what to eat and don't tell me how to talk, okay?"

Mr. Braun narrowed his, I mean, my eyes at me. "You know, Sherman — "

"*Mr. Braun,* to you, dimwad."

He took a deep breath and let it out slowly, as if he were *seething* or something. "You know, someday we're going to switch back. And when we do, you're going to be one very sorry little punk."

I rolled my eyes. Like I was really supposed to be scared? "Dream on, *wuss*."

20

School was cancelled the next day. In the morning, Alex called about shoveling snow, but Mr. Braun begged off. We walked over to his place instead. I don't think he wanted to show me where he lived, but I told him I couldn't stay at my house anymore. It would be too weird for Mr. Braun to sleep there two nights in a row.

"And besides," I said. "My parents will be coming home later. They're gonna think it's really bizarre that my gym teacher is staying over two nights in a row."

Mr. Braun, in my body, smiled like he thought he had the upper hand. "Hey, that's not *my* problem."

"Oh, yeah?" I said. "Well, if you don't let me stay at your place I'll have to sleep in the church basement with the homeless people. And I'll probably wind up getting head lice."

A V formed in Mr. Braun's, I mean, my forehead. "Okay, I'll take you there. But so help me, if you wreck anything I'll — "

"Save it, wuss," I growled.

Mr. Braun lived on the second floor of a two-story garden apartment complex. On the way there he lectured me about how I better take good care of his place and be nice to his neighbors and stuff like that.

Finally we got there. Mr. Braun lived in a one-bedroom apartment. You never saw anyplace so neat and clean. Everything was exactly where it was supposed to be. Muscle magazines with covers of unnaturally muscular men and women were piled neatly on the coffee table. The kitchen was clean and shiny. About twenty large bottles of pills were lined up on the counter. Mr. Braun went over all of them for me.

"These are your amino acids," he said. "Here's your lactose-free whey protein. This is your beta carotene, vitamin B twelve, E, C, and bioflavonoids. Here you've got your iron, zinc, potassium, magnesium, calcium, and boron. And here . . ."

He suddenly stopped. A semi-goofy look came over his, I mean, my face. "Kind of sounds like I eat the natural resources of Montana every morning, doesn't it?"

I wasn't sure if he was kidding or not. "Does all this stuff really come from Montana?"

Mr. Braun scowled at me. "Uh, forget it, Sherman. The point is, as long as you're in my body, this is what you have to take every day. And this is what you're going to eat."

He opened his refrigerator, which was filled with vegetables, fruits, whole grain breads, and junk like that. Then he gave me this big lecture on how, if I was going to use his body, I had an obligation to eat all this stuff instead of the garbage I normally ate.

"Okay, fine, it's a deal," I said, hoping to get him to leave so I could go out and get some chips and stuff. But Mr. Braun wasn't finished.

"Now we'll go over to the Burn Center," he said.

"Why?"

Mr. Braun pointed at me. "Because this body takes work."

21

On the way over, Mr. Braun explained how he worked out every day after school. It turned out that it was the same place Jessica went to, which was probably why he looked familiar to her. You're allowed to bring a guest once for free, so I went in as him and he went in as my guest, Jake Sherman.

The Burn Center is one of those high-tech gyms with all these machines that look like padded torture racks. The walls are lined with floor-to-ceiling mirrors, and you can watch the TVs that hang from the ceiling or listen to rock music piped through speakers. Walking in was kind of cool, because all these muscle guys and girls knew Mr. Braun and were really friendly. I sort of got the feeling Mr. Braun was respected as one of the more serious and dedicated muscleheads around.

We went into the free weight room where people mostly use barbells and dumbbells. Without being too obvious about it, Mr. Braun, in my body, showed me, in his body, how to do all the exercises. It was pretty cool to pick up those huge bars loaded with weights, and grunt and groan as I lifted them. I felt like a real musclehead which, for the moment at least, was exactly what I was.

"Go for the burn," Mr. Braun urged in a low voice as I bench-pressed *400 pounds*!

"The what?" I grunted, feeling like the veins in my, I mean, Mr. Braun's body were going to burst.

"The burn," he said. "When your muscles build up lactic acid and feel like they're burning. The whole idea is to max out into muscle failure."

"Talk English," I groaned.

"*Speak* English." He corrected me again.

"Whatever . . ."

Two bench presses was all I could do. Mr. Braun patted me on his shoulder. "Good work. Rest."

I sat up and caught my breath. My, I mean, Mr. Braun's heart was pounding. All my, I mean, his muscles were pumped up like the guys on the covers of the muscle magazines. My veins were popping out and my skin was glistening with sweat. The whole affect was totally cool. For one brief shining moment, I felt like Arnold.

Meanwhile, Mr. Braun, in my body, stood in front of a mirror. He rolled up his sleeve and tried to make a muscle. It was really pitiful. I mean, there was hardly *a bump* where the muscle was supposed to be.

He slid his sleeve down and looked totally dejected.

We stayed at the Burn Center for nearly three hours. Almost every time I lifted a weight, a couple of people would stop and watch. Like I was a star or something. It was pretty obvious what being a big muscle guy was all about — it was a giant head trip!

When we finally finished, I really hated to leave. Getting all that attention was a real goof. As Mr. Braun and I left, everyone said good-bye. I felt popular. Meanwhile, Mr. Braun, in my body, stood off to the side with his lips pursed together tightly.

"Ready?" he finally asked, as if he were annoyed at me pretending to be him.

We were going out the door when Amber strolled up wearing a coat and sweatpants. She looked surprised to see me and Mr. Braun together.

"Uh, hi, Mr. Braun, hi, Jake," she said. "I've never seen you here before."

Mr. Braun, in my body, didn't say anything because he thought she was talking to me. Actually, she *was* talking to me, but since he was in my body, she was talking to him.

Amber frowned while she waited for Jake to answer.

"Hey, Sherman," I said. "She's talking to you."

"Huh? Oh . . . yeah." Mr. Braun, in my body,

seemed distracted. "Uh, Mr. Braun brought me here today. I'm going to start working out."

Amber smiled. "That's great."

"So maybe he'll see you here, sometime," I said to Amber.

"That would be neat," Amber said.

Since Amber was going in, and we were leaving, we said good-bye. We started to walk along the sidewalk. It was a sunny day. The ground, buildings and cars were covered with a foot of fresh white snow. As we walked, Mr. Braun, in my body, hardly said a thing. Once again, it seemed as if he was *thinking*.

I was thinking too. This was totally unlike the time I switched bodies with Mr. Dirksen, or got stuck in the first day of school. When those things happened, I couldn't wait to get back to normal. But this was different. This time I really *liked* it.

22

The next week was a blast. The science fair ended and they moved the tables out of the gym. I'd planned to let the kids goof off during gym, but from the moment I took over my first class, I made those kids work their tails off. Maybe it was a power trip or just my way of getting back at Mr. Braun now that he was in my body. Every period they ran relays and wind sprints, climbed ropes, and did push-ups, pull-ups, and sit-ups until they were sprawled on the floor, exhausted. Meanwhile, I put a TV in the gym office so I'd have something to watch in my spare time.

The only real problem was food. Mr. Braun's body was always hungry. I finally solved that by going to the Food Warehouse and getting a bunch of those huge bags of chips, pretzels, and other junk.

Rap! Rap! I was in the gym office, watching a talk show, when someone knocked on the door. It was just before the last period of the day. In a few moments, my old gym class would be coming in. They were my favorites.

"Come in," I said without taking my eyes off the TV.

Josh pushed open the door. One of the highlights of the week had been making him hustle until his face turned bright red and he collapsed each day on the wrestling mats in total exhaustion.

"What's up, Hopka?" My feet were up on the desk and I was munching on a bag of bright orange corn twirls.

"Uh, I have a note." Josh slid a white envelope across the desk.

I tore it open and read, " 'Dear Mr. Braun. Please excuse Josh from gym class today. Last night he clipped his toenails too short and his toes are sore.' "

I gave Josh a scornful look. "Get off it."

"It's true, Mr. Braun," he said. "They're really sore."

I pointed at the locker room. "Get in there and get changed before you give me twenty."

"But I've got a note!" Josh pleaded.

"I don't care if you have the United States Constitution!" I growled. "You're taking class!"

Josh screwed up his face angrily, but instead of saying anything, he looked around the office. His eyes stopped at the TV. "You never had a TV in here before."

"Well, aren't you observant," I grumbled. "Now make like a rain forest and disappear."

Josh was hardly out the door when Amber Sweeny came in with a note asking that she be excused from class. Her mom didn't want Amber to get her hair messed up that day.

"What's that all about?" I asked.

Amber blushed a little. "Well, there's this photographer in town who says he wants to try me in a newspaper ad for Berger's department store. He's going to take some pictures of me after school today and my mom's worried that if I get all sweaty in gym I won't look good."

"I see," I said.

"I mean, just between you and me, Mr. Braun, I think she's being pretty silly. I'm sure I could fix up my hair at the photographer's studio. It wouldn't be a big deal."

"No, no, it's important that you look your best," I said. "You're excused."

The next person was Andy, who limped in on crutches with a note saying that he'd slipped on an icy step the night before and twisted his ankle.

"That's too bad," I said.

"Yeah, it really hurts," he said.

"Get changed into your gym clothes," I said.

Andy stared at me like I was out of my mind.

"Got a problem, Kent?" I asked.

"I can't take gym," he said. "I'm on crutches."

"You're excused from running, but you can still

do sit-ups and push-ups." I turned back to the talk show.

Andy's jaw dropped. He just stood there.

"Catching flies, Kent?" I asked without looking away from the TV.

Andy shook his head and limped toward the door. But just before he went out, he stopped. "Know what, Mr. Braun?"

"What?"

"You've gotten really mean." Then he went out.

I stared at the TV, but I was thinking about what he'd said. Maybe I had gotten mean. The funny thing was, it felt *good*.

23

A moment later I turned off the TV and went out into the gym. Kids had started to come out of the locker rooms in their gym clothes. The last few stragglers dashed out carrying their sneakers. I'd made a new rule. Anyone who couldn't change in two minutes had to give me a push-up for every five seconds they were late.

And guess who was late?

"Give me six, Sherman," I barked as Mr. Braun, in my body, jogged out of the locker room thirty seconds late.

"But Ms. Rogers kept me after class," he said.

"Got a late pass?"

Mr. Braun shook my head.

"Then on the floor."

Mr. Braun got down on the gym floor and did six pitiful push-ups. My back dipped like an old horse's and he could barely straighten my arms. I couldn't believe what a wimp I looked like.

"Okay, class," I said. "Today we'll continue our fitness program with wind sprints, push-ups, and sit-ups. And just for fun we'll end the class with a crab walk relay race."

The whole class groaned. By then Mr. Braun had finished his push-ups. He raised my hand.

"What is it now, Sherman?" I asked.

"Yesterday after class I read the physical education curriculum," he said. "It says that we're supposed to be doing badminton this week."

"Badminton is for wimps," I said.

"That's not exactly correct," he said. "It's good for hand-eye coordination and it's an excellent introduction to racket sports."

"Thank you for that enlightening information," I grumbled. "Everybody up for wind sprints."

With a lot of muttering and grumbling, the class stood up. Julia Saks raised her hand.

"Yes, Julia?" I called on her.

"Aren't we supposed to stretch before we start any intensive physical activity?" she asked.

"How thoughtless of me!" I cried. "Okay, class, Julia will now lead you in stretching."

They stretched for a couple of minutes and then started running. Amber was sitting on the bleachers so I went over and sat down next to her.

"So, uh, have you done a lot of modeling?" I asked.

Amber shook her head. "Not really."

"Are you nervous?"

"I feel funny, but I don't think it's nervousness," she said.

"Then what is it?"

"I guess I'm just not sure I really like the idea," Amber said. "My mom says they'll pay me a lot of money if they decide to use me for the ad. But it's not like I'm doing anything to earn it. I mean, it's not like I learned a skill or anything. All you basically have to do is *stand* there."

"What's wrong with that?" I asked.

"The only reason they want me is because of the way I look. It feels really superficial."

"I know what you mean." I nodded.

Amber gave me a funny look. "Do you?"

"Sure," I said. "People shouldn't care about what you look like. It's what's inside that counts."

"If you really feel that way, why did you work so hard to have such big muscles?" she asked.

"Uh . . ." I didn't know what to say.

"I don't mean to be rude or anything, Mr. Braun," Amber went on, "but don't you lift all those weights because you think it makes your body look cool?"

"It's more than that," I tried to explain. "It's eating good healthy food, and iron, zinc, and po-tassium . . . uh, from Montana."

Amber scowled at me. "Can't you eat good healthy food without needing to grow big muscles?"

"Uh . . ."

Just then a commotion broke out over by the rope climbing area. The kids had finished the wind sprints and had broken up into smaller group activities. I got up and went over. To tell you the truth, I wasn't sorry to leave Amber. I got the feeling she didn't like Mr. Braun that much.

A bunch of kids were standing around in a circle.

"I'll get you for this," A familiar voice threatened from inside the circle.

"You? That's a laugh," another familiar voice chuckled.

I pushed through the circle and found Mr. Braun, in my body, pointing at Barry Dunn. "He did an air hanky on me."

"Did not!" Dunn shouted back.

An angry spark appeared in my, I mean, Mr. Braun's eye. "Yes, you did."

"Oh, yeah?" Dunn grumbled. "Then where's the evidence?"

Mr. Braun threw my hands up in disgust.

"See?" Barry Dunn gloated. "You got no proof."

"Then it was spit," Mr. Braun said.

"Okay, okay, what happened?" I asked.

They both started to talk at the same time. Basically it sounded like Dunn had been up on the rope and Mr. Braun had been below and some liquid had hit him in the head.

"It must've been sweat," Dunn said.

"Bull!" Mr. Braun growled. "It was either flying

goobers or spit. Or maybe you were just drooling, you dumb ape."

"Why you!" Dunn charged Mr. Braun, but I stepped in the way.

"That's enough you two," I said. "Come with me."

"Where?" Mr. Braun, in my body, asked.

"We'll settle this like *men*." I led them over to the equipment closet. Inside were some old boxing gloves, and the protective head gear boxers wear when they spar. I gave them each a set.

"Cool!" Dunn had a big, mean leer on his face. He slipped the gloves on and went off to find a friend to lace them up.

Meanwhile, Mr. Braun, in my body, looked appalled. "What are you doing?"

"I think it's time you stood up to Dunn," I said. "If you don't stand up to him, he's just going to pick on you forever."

Mr. Braun clenched his jaw firmly. Just when it looked like he was going to get really peeved, he suddenly relaxed. A small smile even appeared on his face, almost like a smirk.

"Serves me right," he said with an ironic chuckle. "I must say, *Mr. Braun*, you've developed a wry sense of revenge."

Was it my imagination, or was his vocabulary improving?

24

Over in the corner of the gym some wrestling mats were spread out on the floor, covering about the same area as a boxing ring. Dunn was waiting there, tapping his gloves together and bouncing on his toes like a professional boxer. Mr. Braun, in my body, walked toward him, and I followed.

"Excuse me, Mr. Braun."

I turned and found Amber behind me. "Yes?"

"Why are you doing this?" Her brow was furrowed and she looked angry and upset.

"Because Dunn's going to keep picking on kids until someone stands up to him," I said.

"And you really think that by giving him a chance to beat up Jake he's going to learn his lesson?" Amber asked skeptically.

"We'll have to see," I said.

Amber didn't answer. She just stared daggers at me.

Julia Saks came up and blocked my path. "I don't think you're allowed to do this, Mr. Braun."

"I won't let anyone get hurt," I said.

"How are you going to do that?" she asked.

I didn't answer. All I could think about was how I was going to get my revenge for all those times when Mr. Braun called me a wuss and put me down because I wouldn't stand up to Dunn.

Dunn and Mr. Braun had already taken corners on the mat. The rest of the gym class stood around the edges. I stepped into the middle of the mat and motioned the boxers to step forward. Mr. Braun, in my body, and Dunn came to the middle and faced each other.

"Okay, boys, fight clean," I said. "No hitting below the belt. No head butts. When I tell you to break, you break."

Both boys nodded and went back to their corners.

"Okay!" I clapped my hands together. "Round one!"

Dunn bounded across the mats toward Mr. Braun, who held up his gloves and waited, almost impassively. Dunn took a big swing at Mr. Braun's, I mean, my head. Just when it looked as if he was going to cream him, Mr. Braun ducked and punched Dunn in the side, making him double over and grimace for a second.

A big cheer went up around the mat. It seemed as if almost everyone was rooting for me, I mean, Mr. Braun.

After getting hit, Dunn backed away from me with a surprised look on his face.

Then he got serious.

I ended the bout when Mr. Braun's, I mean, my nose started to bleed. Mr. Braun had put up a heroic fight, but he was no match for Dunn, who left the mats with his arms raised triumphantly and a big smile on his face, even though everyone was booing him.

Andy ran into the bathroom and got a couple of ice packs to keep the swelling down. Then he, Josh, and Alex walked with Mr. Braun back to the locker room. Mr. Braun walked with my head held high. He must have been hurting, but he wouldn't let it show.

"Boy, you sure have gotten brave, Jake," Andy told him, and for once he wasn't joking.

"Yeah," agreed Josh. "I can't believe how you hung in there, Jake. That was *really* awesome."

The rest of the kids went to change out of their gym clothes. Suddenly the gym was empty and quiet. Everyone was gone except for me and Amber. She was still glaring at me with fury in her eyes. It made me feel so uncomfortable that I told her to go ahead to her next class.

"This is the last class of the day, Mr. Braun," she replied coldly.

Oh, right. *How could I have forgotten?*

"Feel good?" Amber asked angrily.

Actually, I didn't feel good at all. But I wouldn't admit that to *her*.

"Think Barry Dunn is going to stop picking on kids now?" Amber's voice was filled with acid scorn. I felt like she was pushing the limits of the student-teacher relationship.

"I'd watch your mouth," I warned her. "Don't forget who's the teacher and who's the student."

"Maybe it's just getting hard to tell," Amber shot back. Then she turned and stormed out of the gym.

25

The vegetables in Mr. Braun's refrigerator were getting moldy, and I hadn't touched any of those vitamins or minerals either. After munching on snacks all day, I usually had a pizza for dinner. Before I'd gotten into Mr. Braun's body, the most slices I could eat at one sitting were three. But in Braun's body I could put away a whole medium-size pie, *with* sausage and mushrooms!

But I was starting to have a problem with his clothes. They'd always been tight, but now they were getting tighter. One morning I discovered I couldn't get the top buttons on any of his pants closed. I had to leave the button open, and wore one of his sweatshirts to school that day, so no one would see.

After school that afternoon I decided to go to the Burn Center. I hadn't been there since the day Mr. Braun took me. I kept meaning to go, but each day after school I'd get back to Mr.

Braun's place, turn on the TV, and order a pizza. Somehow I just never got around to leaving the apartment after that.

The men's and women's locker rooms were in the back of the club. I went into the men's locker room and started pulling off Mr. Braun's street clothes. Suddenly I felt a pair of eyes staring at me. I turned and found Mr. Braun, in my body, wearing a pair of shorts and no shirt. My nose looked a little swollen and a dark crescent curved under my left eye where Dunn had hit me.

Mr. Braun looked really peeved. "What are you doing to my body?" he growled behind clenched teeth.

"What are you talking about?" I pretended not to understand.

Mr. Braun stepped closer and reached toward my waist. He took a fold of flab between his thumb and index finger and pinched it. "I never had *that* before!"

"Get lost." I pushed his hand away.

"It took me fifteen years to build that body," Mr. Braun said angrily. "And in less than two weeks you've let it go to pot."

"Have not."

"You haven't been here once," he said accusingly.

"Have too."

"Liar."

"How would *you* know?" I asked.

"Because *I've* been here every day," he said.

"What?" Since Mr. Braun wasn't wearing a shirt, I gave my body a closer look. Strangely, I could see muscles in places where I'd never seen muscles before. They weren't big, but they were definitely there.

"You've been working out?" I asked.

"Three hours a day." He pulled on a T-shirt.

I couldn't believe it. "Why? That's not even your body."

Mr. Braun shrugged my shoulders. "Habit, I guess."

This was *fantastic*! If Mr. Braun kept it up, I was going to have a great body *without doing any exercises*!

A few moments later we left the locker room together. Out in the weight room, the muscle-heads greeted me. "Hey, Teddy, haven't seen you around lately. Where you been?" "Wow, man, looks like you're overdoing the carbo-loading." "You're not gonna let that body go, are ya, Ted?"

I dealt with their questions as best I could and headed for the sit-up machine.

"What are you doing?" Mr. Braun, in my body, asked.

"Sit-ups." I pinched my, I mean, Mr. Braun's waist. "You know, work a little of this off."

"You better start on a treadmill first," Mr. Braun said. "Burn some calories and get yourself warmed up."

I couldn't believe he was telling me what to do.

"Look, this isn't school, okay?" I said. "I'll do what I want."

"Jake?"

We turned around. Jessica was standing behind us, giving us both a puzzled look.

"Uh, hi, Mr. Braun," she said.

"Hi, Jessica." I hadn't seen her in more than a week. I know it must sound kind of strange, but I sort of missed her a little.

Jessica turned to Mr. Braun, in my body. "Think you could spot me for bench presses, Jake?"

"Sure," Mr. Braun replied. "I just want to get a towel." He headed toward the front counter. Jessica and I waited by the bench press.

"So, uh, how are things at home?" I asked.

Jessica scowled at me as if she couldn't understand why Mr. Braun would ask. "Okay."

"That, uh, dog of yours all right?"

"Lance? Sure, he's fine."

Across the weight room Jake appeared with a towel.

"Looks like Jake's really gotten into working out, huh?" I said.

Jessica nodded. "I'll say. Actually, he's really

changed *a lot* in the past few weeks. It's like he's a completely different person."

"Is the change for better or for worse?" I asked.

"Definitely better," my sister said. "It's like he *finally* decided to grow up."

I grimaced. *Ouch!* That hurt.

26

Mr. Braun, in my body, went to spot my sister on the bench press. I walked over to the treadmills. Three were empty. I got a pair of headphones, climbed up on one of the treadmills, and tossed my towel on the handrail of the one next to me. A row of television monitors hung from the ceiling. At least I'd get to watch TV while I jogged.

A few minutes later, Mr. Braun came by. He must have finished spotting Jessica. He got on the second treadmill, leaving the one between us free. By then I'd started to work up a sweat and stopped jogging.

"Where are you going?" he asked.

"To do sit-ups," I said.

Mr. Braun craned my neck to read the data on my treadmill's electronic display. "Only seven minutes?"

"Hey, I worked up a sweat," I said defensively.

"You've got to jog at least twenty minutes for it to mean anything," he said.

I figured another couple of minutes wouldn't kill me, and got back on the treadmill. Meanwhile, Mr. Braun, in my body, started *running* on his treadmill.

"You know, er, *Mr. Braun*, I was just thinking about something interesting," he said as he ran. "Have you ever wondered why people lift weights and build up their bodies so fanatically?"

"Sure," I said. "They want to look good and feel strong."

"Don't you think that's kind of simplistic?" Mr. Braun asked.

Mr. Braun was asking *me* if something was simplistic? Wow, was *that* a switch or what?

"Well, what do *you* think the answer is?" I asked.

"Everyone knows you get more strength from doing high reps with medium weight, so strength really isn't the issue," Mr. Braun said.

Once again it seemed like he was starting to sound *smarter*!

"So then you have to consider looks," Mr. Braun went on. "Why is it so important to *look* strong? What does it say about people if they have to spend so much of their lives worried about their appearance?"

"Don't ask me," I said, lowering my voice to a

whisper. *"You're* the one who spent fifteen years doing it."

"Right." Mr. Braun didn't get mad like I expected he would. Instead he said, "It seems to me that someone has to be pretty insecure to go through all that trouble just to look strong."

"Whatever you say," I replied. I wasn't keen on all this psychological mumbo jumbo.

"Is this treadmill taken?" someone asked.

I turned and came face-to-face with Amber. She was pointing at the treadmill between Mr. Braun and me.

I reached over and pulled my towel off the rail. "It's yours."

"Thanks." Amber stepped up on the treadmill. I was glad she was there, because I felt like we'd parted on bad terms after gym class that day. Amber started jogging and scanned the TV shows on the monitors. But just as I turned to talk to her, she turned to Mr. Braun in my body.

"How are you, Jake?" she asked.

It seemed like she caught him by surprise. "Oh, uh, you mean the nose? It's just a little swollen."

"I thought you were really brave to fight that jerk," Amber said.

"Well, it wasn't like I had a *choice*," Mr. Braun said loudly, like he wanted to make sure I heard. Amber gave me an unfriendly look and turned back to him.

"I really wish there was *something* someone

could do about that bully," she said.

Mr. Braun, in my body, nodded.

"It's really too bad the school doesn't do something about him," Amber said. Again I got the feeling she said it so I could hear.

"There's just so much they can do," Mr. Braun replied. "Dunn's a pain, but he isn't really a threat. It's not like he seriously *injures* people."

"I guess," Amber said. "I just don't understand why Principal Blanco doesn't suspend him or something. Then he'd stop."

"Dunn doesn't care if he gets suspended," I said. "And Principal Blanco doesn't know how bad it is because most of the kids won't tell him. They don't want to look like crybabies."

"So why don't *you* tell Principal Blanco?" Amber asked.

Oops! For a moment there I'd forgotten whose body I was in.

"Or better yet, the next time Dunn spits on Jake, instead of making Jake fight him, why don't you punish Dunn?" Amber added sharply.

"But I didn't see him spit," I tried to explain.

"Oh, please, Mr. Braun." Amber scoffed. "Do you think Jake really made that up?"

She had a good point. Still, I knew there had to be a reasonable argument. If only I could *think* of it.

Just then the front door to the health club swung open and Josh and Andy came in. That caught me totally by surprise. I almost asked what they were doing there when I realized that it probably wasn't something Mr. Braun would normally ask.

They headed straight for the treadmills.

"Hey, Jake, is it true?" Andy gasped excitedly.

Mr. Braun quickly put my finger to my lips. "Shhhhhh!" He nodded at me. Andy and Josh glanced my way and got the message. Whatever was going on, Mr. Braun didn't want me to know about it.

"What is it?" Amber gasped, leaning toward them.

Josh whispered something in her ear. Unfortunately, with the music playing and everyone around us exercising, she couldn't hear.

"What?" she said.

Josh raised his voice. "I said, Jake challenged The Dunce to a rematch."

Everyone looked at me. Then Mr. Braun, in my body, glared at Josh, who bit his lip and looked totally guilty.

"Oops, sorry," he said sheepishly.

"Really?" Amber gasped.

Mr. Braun acted as if it were no big deal. Amber's eyes went wide. She was looking at him in my body as if he were some kind of hero. Andy and Josh were looking at him the same way. I hate to say it, but I was starting to feel really jealous.

Only, how could I be jealous of myself?

27

It was two days until Christmas vacation. The joy of making all the kids in school kill themselves in gym was starting to wear thin, and living in Mr. Braun's apartment made me feel lonely. And I had some other problems.

One was that I'd started to feel really thick-skulled. It was a serious challenge just to *think*. Coming up with ideas and solving problems used to be easy for me, but now using my brain was like trudging through thick drifts of heavy, wet snow.

The other problem was that Bertha had called from the Ms. Galaxy Pageant in California. She talked about how much she missed me and how she'd be home very soon.

I hated to admit it, but even though I was in Mr. Braun's big strong body, the prospect of seeing his beautiful girlfriend made me nervous.

It was the last period of school and my old gym class was changing in the locker rooms. Everyone hurried out to the gym. When the bell rang, I looked around and realized only one person was missing, Jake Sherman.

Half a minute passed, then a minute. Then two minutes.

At two minutes and fifteen seconds, Mr. Braun, in my body, raced out of the boys' locker room. He didn't even wait for me to say anything. Instead, he got down on the floor and proceeded to do twenty-seven perfect push-ups. One for every five seconds of lateness.

When he finished, a bunch of kids cheered. Mr. Braun, in my body, stood up and waved at them with a big smile on his face. He wasn't even *winded*.

The funny thing was, I wouldn't have made him do those push-ups this time. Like I said, I was tired of being Mr. Mean.

"So what are we gonna do today, Mr. Braun?" Howie Jamison asked.

"Why bother asking, bonehead?" Alex Silver chastised him. "You know it'll be the same thing we always do. Sprints, push-ups, sit-ups, the whole nine yards."

"Wrong." I shook my head. "Actually, today I'm giving you a free period. Play basketball, fool around, talk to your friends, whatever you like."

Forty kids stared back at me with shocked looks on their faces.

"Is this a joke, Mr. Braun?" Andy asked.

"No, but I want to see you and Hopka in my office."

"Why?" Josh asked. "What'd we do?"

"Nothing." I turned and went into the office. Inside, I sat down at the desk, turned on the TV, and ripped open a new bag of chips. Through the window I could see that a bunch of kids had gotten out a basketball and were playing a half-court game. Others were sitting around talking. Only one kid elected to do the sprints we normally did —Mr. Braun, in my body.

Andy and Josh came into the office looking nervous. "Want some?" I held the open bag of chips toward them. My friends shared a frown, then each reached into the bag, felt around for a good-size chip, and took it out.

"Uh, thanks, Mr. Braun," Josh said uncertainly as he munched on his chip.

"Have a seat," I said.

With puzzled looks on their faces, they sat down in the chairs on the other side of my desk. I slid a cassette of *Terminator 2* into the VCR. It felt good to be sitting around with my pals again, eating junk food and watching Schwarzenegger mash bad guys.

I held the bag out again. "More?"

"Uh, sure, thanks." Josh and Andy each took another chip.

"Uh, excuse me, Mr. Braun," Andy said. "But is there a *reason* why you wanted to see us?"

I reached into the bag and pulled out a handful of chiplets. "Not really."

Out in the gym, Jake had finished with his wind sprints. Now he was sitting on the floor with his knees bent. Alex Silver held his ankles while he did dozens of rapid, effortless sit-ups. Not far away, Barry Dunn stood with one of his friends, watching. Dunn's forehead was wrinkled. He actually looked worried.

"Can you believe Sherman?" I asked with a smile. I was turning back to watch the movie when I noticed that both Josh and Andy were staring at me wide-eyed, as if they'd suddenly realized something.

They looked back out the window at Mr. Braun, in my body, exercising as hard as he could.

Then they looked at me in Mr. Braun's body with my feet up on the desk, munching on a handful of chiplets and watching the movie.

Uh-oh! I suddenly realized what I'd done. Sitting up, I quickly wiped my hands on Mr. Braun's sweatpants. Then, trying to sound more like Mr. Braun than Mr. Braun himself, I said, "All right, boys. Better get moving."

But my friends didn't move. They just looked at me and then at each other.

"You thinking what I'm thinking?" Andy asked Josh.

Josh nodded. "Yeah, suddenly it's all starting to make sense."

"What's making sense?" I asked innocently.

"You know," Andy said.

"No, I don't," I said, "but if you're not out on that gym floor in five seconds, you're going to be cleaning the bathroom with a paintbrush . . . er, I mean, a toothbrush."

Andy pointed a finger at me. "Don't go anywhere," he said. "I'll be back."

28

Ten minutes later, Andy hurried back into the office, followed by Jessica. She studied me like I was an alien or something. Andy's face was red and he was panting. I could only imagine that he'd just snuck out of school and run over to the high school to get Jessica.

"It's against the rules to leave this property during school hours," I said. "I'm afraid I'm going to have to report you to Principal Blanco."

"Get stuffed, bozo." Andy turned to my sister. "Tell him what you told me on the way here."

"I said that Jake was acting really different," Jessica said. "Like he was a whole new person."

They looked out the office window at Mr. Braun in my body, who was now doing push-ups. His body was as straight as a board. Then they turned back to me. I'd just put a big handful of chiplets in my mouth.

"And the night of the big snowstorm?" Andy asked Jessica.

My sister told how Mr. Braun had stayed at our house.

"Wait a minute!" Josh gasped. "That was the night before the science fair! Mr. Dirksen's experiment was here in the gym! Alex and Jake stayed late for detention."

"I don't know what you're talking about, Hopka," I said, trying to act tough. Then I pointed to Jessica. "And you don't even belong here."

Andy opened the gym office door and yelled for Alex. A moment later he came in. When he saw Josh and Jessica, he scowled. "What's going on?"

"That's what I'd like to know," I said with as much bluster as I could muster. "You're really in trouble, Kent."

"Just keep your mouth shut," Andy grunted.

"Huh?" Alex's jaw dropped. "Did you just tell Mr. Braun to keep his mouth shut?"

"You ain't seen nothin' yet," Andy glowered. "I can't believe how hard this guy made us work in gym these last few weeks. I could *kill* him."

"Hey, Andy, get a grip," Alex cautioned him.

"Remember that night you and Jake stayed in the gym for detention?" Andy asked Alex.

"Yeah, the night of the big snowstorm," Alex said.

"What'd you do?" Josh asked.

"We helped move Mr. Dirksen's experiment in for the science fair," Alex said.

"Then what?" Jessica asked.

Alex frowned. "I went to wait outside for my mom. Why?"

"Where were Jake and Mr. Braun?" Josh asked.

"In the gym," Alex said.

"Where was Mr. Dirksen?" Andy asked.

"He went home because of the storm."

"So Jake and Mr. Braun were alone in the gym with Mr. Dirksen's experiment?" Jessica asked.

"Yeah, why?"

"Did anything weird happen?" Andy asked.

Alex thought for a moment. "Well, actually, yes. First there was a power failure, then some kind of explosion."

"Explosion?" Jessica gasped.

"Yeah," Alex said. "Then my mom came and I went to get them. Jake and Mr. Braun were having a fight. Then Mr. Braun went home with Jake. Why? What's this all about?"

Andy just shook his head. "Thanks, man, you can go."

"Aren't you gonna tell me what's going on?" Alex asked.

"You'd never believe us." Andy showed Alex to the office door and closed it behind him. Then he turned back to me. "You low-life phlegmwad . . . making us do all those wind sprints and push-ups."

"Those crab walk races," Josh added.

"Pull-ups!" Andy grumbled.

"Sit-ups!" Josh said angrily.

94

Jessica pointed out the window at Mr. Braun, in my body. "I can't *believe* I let that man see me in my *pajamas*!"

Josh pointed an accusing finger at me. "You made me take gym with sore toes."

"Hey, forget it," I said. "That was the lamest excuse ever."

"You made *me* take gym with a twisted ankle," Andy growled. "I was on crutches."

"You healed, didn't you?" I said, reaching into the bag of chips and taking out another handful of chiplets.

"Gimme that!" Josh snatched the bag away from me.

"I'm gonna get you for this, Jake," Andy threatened.

"Hey, *bozo*, as far as everyone else is concerned, I'm still your gym teacher," I said. "You try to tell Principal Blanco I switched bodies with Mr. Braun and you're gonna wind up in some psycho ward somewhere."

Andy drummed his fingers on Mr. Braun's desk, then turned to Josh and Jessica. "Listen, guys. Mr. Dirksen moved the experiment into his room here at school. Tomorrow's the last day before Christmas vacation. If we're gonna switch them back, it's got to be tomorrow."

I listened in amazement as my sister and my two best friends came up with a plan. They all agreed that they'd have to tell Mr. Dirksen, and that the best time to make the switch would be at the end of the day. Half the school would be gone by then and the other half would be so preoccupied with getting out that they probably wouldn't even notice that something out of the ordinary was going on. The way they were talking, you would have thought I wasn't even in the room.

"Wait a minute, guys," I finally said. "Has it occurred to any of you that I might not *want* to switch back to my old body?"

Josh, Jessica, and Andy looked at each other.

"He's got a point," my sister said. "Frankly, I like the new Jake a lot more than the old one. All I have to do is start wearing a robe."

"Gee, thanks," I said with a sniff.

Andy shook his head. "You're switching back, Jake. There's *no way* you're gonna be my gym teacher for the rest of the year."

"You can't make me," I said.

The three of them grew quiet. Then Josh shook his head slowly. "No wonder Jake had the guts to fight The Dunce. I should've realized right then that he wasn't the same wuss I've known all these years."

That really ticked me off. Who did they think they were? After all, if I wanted to, I could be Mr. Braun *forever*. I could bench press 400 pounds! I had a girlfriend who'd just competed in the Ms. Galaxy Pageant! With one hand tied behind my back, I could demolish all three of them, *and* Barry Dunn!

Josh started to stick his hand into *my* bag of chips. I leaned over the desk and grabbed it away. "That's it!" I barked. "All of you, *get out!*"

29

That night in Mr. Braun's apartment I ordered a pizza and watched TV. I was still really ticked. I didn't have to switch back if I didn't want to, and they couldn't make me. I didn't care *who* they told. No one was going to believe them. And even if someone did, it was tough noogies.

Ding dong! The doorbell rang. Figuring it was the pizza delivery, I answered it.

But the pizza delivery guy wasn't standing outside. Bertha was. I'd forgotten about her.

"Teddy!" Her eyes got watery and she threw her arms around my neck and hugged me.

I swallowed nervously and backed out of her grasp. "Oh, uh, hi, Bertha, how was the pageant?"

Bertha shook her head sadly and started to unbutton her coat. "The same old problem, Teddy."

I watched her unbutton the coat. Oddly, it looked about five sizes too big.

"What problem?" I asked.

"The judges always criticize me for extreme

muscularity." Bertha pulled off her coat. "They're so sexist. They just can't deal with a woman with lots of hard, dense muscle."

Bertha tossed her coat on the couch. I felt my jaw drop. She was . . . *totally muscle bound*! From the neck up, she was definitely attractive, but from the neck down she had the biggest muscles I'd ever seen on any woman *anywhere*!

"Wha . . . what kind of pageant is Ms. Galaxy?" I stammered.

Bertha scowled. "A body-building competition. You know that, Teddy."

"Uh . . ."

"Is something wrong?" Looking worried, Bertha stepped toward me.

"Uh . . ." I stepped back. There was no way I could deal with this. *No way!* The next thing I knew, two mammoth muscular arms went around me and squeezed so hard that I could hardly breathe.

"Hey, come on, honey," she whispered in my ear, sending a shiver down my spine. "It's me, Bertha, your big mushy wooshy lovey poo."

Suddenly it was time to switch bodies.

30

"There must have been a power surge when the emergency generator kicked in," Mr. Dirksen said as he fiddled with the dials on the experiment. Jessica, Josh, Andy, Mr. Braun in my body, and I were in the science lab. It was the last period of school before Christmas vacation.

"How come you suddenly changed your mind?" Andy asked me.

"Uh . . ." I glanced out of the corner of my eye at Mr. Braun, in my body. "Bertha came home last night."

"And?" Mr. Braun raised my eyebrows curiously.

"Let's just say she was really happy to see me . . . er, I mean, *you*."

Mr. Braun squinted my eyes suspciously.

"She's a very nice person," I added quickly. "I can see how you two have a lot in common."

Meanwhile, Jessica was looking up at the clock over the lab door. "Five minutes left, Mr. Dirksen. We better hurry. You know what happens the second school's over."

"I'm hurrying," Mr. Dirksen replied. "I just want to make sure everything's in order before we begin."

As soon as the last bell rang, everyone who was still at school was going to bolt like wild horses out of a corral. Mr. Blanco and the janitors would come around and shut the place down as fast as they could.

Jessica turned to me. "I hope you've learned something from this experience."

"Sure," I said. "The bigger you are, the more pizza you can eat."

Jessica rolled her eyes. "Figures."

"I've learned quite a lot, actually," said Mr. Braun, in my body. "In fact, this experience has caused me to reassess my entire philosophy of life. Quite frankly, I've come to realize that there must be some higher purpose to our existence than simply striving for big muscles. If you consider the western existential philosophers, then perhaps having big muscles *is* as legitimate as any other pursuit. But if you take a more Darwinian outlook, specifically that we should endeavor to enhance the species for the sake of future generational survival, well, that certainly brings into question such an egocentric pursuit as body building."

Josh scrunched up his face. "What is he talking about?"

"Don't ask me." Jessica shook her head wearily. "But it's really starting to get annoying. Last night he went on for hours about the nature of the universe. I was just about ready to barf."

"That's really not an acceptable word, Jessica," Mr. Braun, in my body, corrected her. "Regurgitate would be a more fitting description."

Jessica turned to Mr. Dirksen. "Would you *please* switch them back *now*?"

"I think we're ready," Mr. Dirksen replied.

"I hope so," Andy said, eyeing the clock. "There's less than a minute left before school ends."

"All right," Mr. Dirksen said. "Mr. Braun and Jake, take your positions. Josh, please turn off the lights."

"Why, Mr. Dirksen?" Josh asked as he went to the light switch by the door.

"We're going to need every ounce of energy we can draw," Mr. Dirksen explained.

Josh flicked the light switch off and the room became dim. Mr. Dirksen turned some knobs and his experiment began to hum.

"All right now," he said, peering at some dials. "Just a few more moments . . ."

Buzzzzzz! The final school bell rang.

"Uh oh!" Andy gasped.

"Don't worry, Kent." Mr. Dirksen peered at the dials. The whirring sound was growing louder.

"It'll just take another moment. Four . . . three . . . two . . . one!"

I felt a slight jolt.

Then the door to the lab opened. Principal Blanco stepped in and flicked the light switch on.

Whhuuuummmmppp!

Everything went black.

31

I opened my eyes.

I was lying on my back, on the cold hard floor of the science lab. Everything was spinning, but I managed to focus on the ring of faces staring down at me with awestruck expressions. Mr. Dirksen, Jessica, Principal Blanco, Andy, Josh, and Mr. Braun. When I saw Mr. Braun's face, I relaxed.

We'd made the switch!

"Jake, are you okay?" Jessica gasped.

"I think so." Still feeling dizzy, I pushed myself up to a sitting position. "I guess I must've fainted or something."

The others shared a worried look.

"Oh, my gosh!" Mr. Braun gasped. "No! This can't be true!"

"What is it?" I asked, still trying to shake the cobwebs out of my head.

"It didn't work," Andy said.

"Sure it did," I said, pointing at Mr. Braun. "He's Mr. Braun and I'm . . ."

My words trailed off as I focused on the arm I was pointing with. It was a huge, muscular arm. I knew Mr. Braun had been exercising my body really hard, but there was no way I could have grown muscles as big as *these*.

I looked at Mr. Braun, who was looking down at his body.

Only it wasn't *his* body.

It was mine.

32

"What's going on in here?" Principal Blanco demanded. He focused on me and scowled. "What happened to *you*, Sherman?"

Somehow, only our heads had switched. Mine was now on Mr. Braun's body, and vice versa. I glanced at Mr. Dirksen, who shook his head furiously. He didn't want me to tell the principal what had happened. I had a feeling I knew why. Principals probably took a dim view of teachers who used their students as guinea pigs in science experiments.

"I, uh, I've been working out really hard," I said.

"You don't say?" Principal Blanco arched his eyebrow skeptically. "I'm sure you're aware of the dangers of steroid use, Sherman."

"Principal Blanco, I can vouch for the fact that Jake has *never* even seen a steroid," Jessica interrupted. "He's been on a new fitness regimen, and it's had *amazing* results."

"I'll say." Principal Blanco turned to Mr. Braun, who was still staring down at my body, looking crushed. "And what happened to *you*, Ted?"

"I . . . I . . ." Mr. Braun didn't know what to say. Behind Principal Blanco, Mr. Dirksen was still waving his arms frantically and shaking his head.

"I've been on this crash diet," Mr. Braun finally said.

Principal Blanco scratched his head, then looked at his watch. "I don't know what's going on here, but I'm taking my family down to Disney World in a few hours. We've got a six o'clock flight, and I have to close up the school first. So all of you have to clear out immediately."

"But!" Mr. Dirksen and Mr. Braun gasped simultaneously.

"No buts," Principal Blanco stated firmly. "School is officially closed for Christmas vacation. None of you are supposed to be here. So get going."

We picked up our stuff and, in a group, walked out through the main entrance of school.

Bang! One of the janitors slammed the door behind us and locked it. A moment later all the lights inside went off.

We stood silently on the curb and watched as Principal Blanco walked across the parking lot to his car. He paused for a second and looked back at us with a puzzled expression on his face. Then he shook his head, got in, and drove away. A moment later the janitors also got into their cars and left.

The sky was gray and getting dark. The trees were bare and still in the windless air. As we stood outside in the cold, I wondered what was on TV that night.

"Now what?" Jessica asked.

"There's nothing we can do," Mr. Dirksen said hopelessly. "We'll just have to wait until after vacation. I propose that on the first day back, Jake, Ted, and I get to school half an hour early. We'll have to complete the switch then."

Mr. Braun spread my arms. "I have to go through the whole vacation looking like *this*?"

"It's not such a bad body," I said. "You've really improved it."

"Meanwhile, you've let *my* body go to flab," Mr. Braun said angrily.

"Have not." I made a muscle. "Feel that. It's still solid rock."

Josh felt the muscle and nodded. "It's pretty hard."

"Well, if you're going to have my body all vacation, try not to let it get any worse, okay?" Mr. Braun snapped. "Cut out all the junk food and get into the gym a couple of hours a day."

"What if I don't?" I asked.

"You'll be real sorry when we finally do switch bodies completely."

But I wasn't so sure.

33

"What happened to *you*?" my mother gasped that night when I came down for dinner. It was the first time in weeks that she and Dad had gotten home early enough to eat with Jessica and me.

My father looked up from his newspaper, and his eyes bugged out. "Jake? Are you all right?"

"Sure. I've been working out." I took a seat at the kitchen table.

Mom and Dad gaped at each other. Then Dad knitted his eyebrows.

"Have you been taking steroids?" he asked.

"No way," I said.

"He's been working out really hard," Jessica said, coming into the kitchen. "Two or three hours every day after school and on the weekends."

"I understand," Dad said, still staring at me. "But, you're *huge*."

Normally I would have come back with a snappy reply, but lately my brain always felt like it was on empty.

110

"Well, you know what they say," Jessica said quickly. "The teenage years are times of great change."

Mom and Dad were pretty flabbergasted, but there wasn't much they could do except ask more questions. The person they were talking to was definitely their son . . . at least from the neck up.

I'd just finished dinner (including seconds *and* thirds) when the doorbell rang.

"I'll get it." I jumped up and went to the front door. Josh and Andy were outside.

"Hey, big guy," Andy said, "feel like catching a movie at the mall?"

"Huh?" I didn't understand what they were doing there. "Aren't you guys mad at me?"

"You bet we are," Josh said.

"But you also got us into better shape than we've been in for years," Andy added. "And besides, now that you're gargantuan, we want to be seen with you."

Andy grinned and winked. I winked back. I missed hanging out with my friends. "Okay. I'll get my coat."

"Shouldn't you ask your parents first?" Josh asked.

"Uh . . ." I hadn't thought of that. "I guess I should, huh?"

"Naw," said Andy. "When you have giant muscles you don't have to *ask* anybody."

"I don't?" Now I was confused. Was he serious or kidding?

"Let's just go," Andy said with a sigh.

We got to the mall early and went into the music store to kill some time before the movie began. After wandering up and down the aisles for a few minutes, Andy suddenly nudged me.

"Hey, look," he whispered.

A few rows over, Barry Dunn was browsing around in the heavy metal section.

Josh joined us. "Want to goof on him?"

"How?" I whispered.

We huddled and Josh outlined his plan. It was kind of complicated.

"Could you repeat the last part?" I asked him when he was done.

"Why?"

"It was a little hard to follow."

Josh and Andy scowled at each other. Then Josh went over the plan again.

"Now, are you *sure* you understand?" he whispered when he was done.

"Yeah," I whispered back. "Pretty sure."

"Okay," he whispered. "Get into position."

Unfortunately, I'd forgotten what my position was.

"Over *here*, Jake," Andy hissed. He and Josh were hiding behind a tall display of CDs. I joined them and crouched down so that only my head was visible above the display. Josh and Andy weren't visible at all.

"Get his attention," Andy whispered.

"Whose?" I whispered back.

"Dunn's, you dummy!" Josh hissed.

I made a fist. "Who're you calling a dummy?"

"Uh, sorry, Jake." Josh swallowed. "Would you *please* call Barry a dork?"

"Hey, Barry, you dork!" I called across the aisle.

A couple of aisles over, Dunn looked up, surprised. His face hardened when he saw me. All he could see was my head.

"Go on," Andy whispered.

"Go on what?" I whispered back.

"Call him a dimwit, for Pete's sake," Josh hissed.

"You're a dimwit for Pete's sake," I said.

Dunn frowned.

"No!" Andy whispered. "You're not supposed to say for Pete's sake."

"But Josh said I was," I whispered back.

"Tell him he's a headbanger," Josh whispered.

"You're a headbanger," I said.

Dunn narrowed his eyes at me.

"Tell him heavy metal makes you lame," Josh whispered.

"Heavy metal makes me lame," I said.

"No!" Josh hissed. "It makes *him* lame."

"It makes you lame, too," I said to Dunn.

Dunn smirked and nodded as if he understood what I was doing. "Let me guess, Sherman. You're trying to get me mad so I'll pick a fight with you right here."

I looked down at Josh and Andy and whispered, "That's not the plan, is it?"

They both rolled their eyes and groaned.

"Can't wait until after vacation for your rematch, huh?" Dunn grinned, and started toward me. "Okay, geek, let's do it. Just because you've been working out for a couple of weeks doesn't mean you know how to fight."

A moment later Dunn was only one aisle away.

"Okay, go!" Andy whispered.

"Where?" I whispered back.

Instead of answering, Andy and Josh shoved me into the aisle right in front of Barry. He stopped. His eyes bulged and his jaw dropped as he looked at me.

Andy stuck his head up over the CD display. "Still want to fight, Barry?"

Dunn just stared at me. I flexed my muscles the way I'd seen Mr. Braun do it.

"Wha . . ." Dunn stammered. "What happened to you?"

"He ate his Wheaties," Josh said. "Now come on, tough guy, let's see you rumble."

Dunn turned around and ran out of the store.

Josh and Andy burst out laughing and gave each other high fives.

"Did you see that?" Andy cried.

"He was totally freaked!" Josh cackled. "Guess he's not interested in that rematch after all."

"Boy, I sure wish I could have gotten that on tape!" Andy said. "Don't you, Jake?"

"Why?" I asked.

Josh and Andy stopped laughing. For a moment they were both quiet. Josh checked his watch.

"Come on, it's time for the movie," he said.

34

Before the movie started, Josh bought a container of popcorn for the three of us to share. But halfway through the previews it seemed like he got mad. He left and came back with a giant-size popcorn which he said was just for me. I thought that was really nice of him.

Afterwards we decided to get some pizza.

"So what'd you think of the movie?" Andy asked as we walked through the mall toward the food court.

"Totally excellent," Josh said. "What did you think, Jake?"

"It was okay," I said.

"Just okay?" Josh looked puzzled.

"Well, I didn't understand why the guy with the green hat cut the phone cables," I said.

"Because he was secretly working for the bad guys," Andy said. "I mean, that was *obvious*."

"And what about the girl with the long black hair?" I asked. "She was supposed to be working for the bad guys. How come she saved the hero?"

"Because she had a change of heart," Josh said. "She decided the good guy was right. That was the whole point of the story."

"Oh!" Now it made more sense to me. "I think I get it."

Josh and Andy shared a funny look. Then Andy sighed and mumbled something about the "old Jake," but I didn't quite understand what he meant.

We got to the pizza place, and were just about to go in when Mr. Braun came out with Bertha. Josh and Andy looked at Mr. Braun's muscular girlfriend and had the same reaction I'd had when I first met her.

"Oh, hi, Mr. Braun," Andy said after he'd recovered. "What are you doing here?"

Mr. Braun didn't look real happy to see us. "We just had dinner. Bertha, this is Josh, Andy, and Jake. Three of my students. Guys, this is Bertha."

"Pleased to meet you," Andy said.

"Yeah, Mr. Braun talks about you all the time," added Josh.

You would have expected Bertha to beam proudly, but instead she gave us a taut smile. Her eyes seemed to rest on me.

Just then Mr. Braun blinked as if a lightbulb had gone off in his head. "Know what? They overcharged us! Excuse me boys, I'll be right back."

He went back into the pizza place. Meanwhile,

Bertha looked me over with a warm expression on her face.

"You're one of Teddy's students?" she asked.

"Uh, yeah," I said.

"You didn't get those big muscles in gym class, did you?" she asked.

"Uh . . ." I didn't know what to say.

"He works out over at the Burn Center," Andy said.

"Really?" Bertha looked surprised. "I never saw you there."

"Uh . . ." I still didn't know what to say.

"He usually goes late at night," Josh said.

"Oh, that explains it," Bertha smiled at me again. "Maybe I'll have to start going late at night, too."

Mr. Braun came back out of the pizza place. "I knew it! Our waitress miscalculated the sales tax. She charged us seventy-three cents too much."

"Wow, Teddy, you really grew brains while I was away," Bertha said, sounding a little sarcastic.

Mr. Braun smiled proudly. "Well, we better get going. Have a good vacation, boys." His eyes stayed fixed on me. "I'll see *you* when school reopens."

He and Bertha left.

"Gee, do you believe that?" Andy gasped when they were out of earshot.

"Believe what?" I asked.

"A couple of weeks ago Mr. Braun couldn't figure out what to add to fourteen to get fifty. Now he's doing out sales tax in his head!"

"Who cares about that?" Josh said. "Did you see Bertha? She's built like a refrigerator."

"She lifts weights, too," I said.

Andy gave me a look of disbelief. "No kidding, Einstein."

"Why'd you call me that?" I asked.

"Forget it." Andy shook his head.

"Did you see the way she looked at Jake?" Josh asked.

"You bet I did." Andy looked at me woefully. "I hate to say this, but I think you're in trouble, big guy."

"Why?" I asked.

"First you took Mr. Braun's body," Andy said. "Now you're gonna take his girl."

35

Every day during vacation, I went to the Burn Center and worked out. Now that it was *my* head on Mr. Braun's body, I really wanted to take good care of the whole unit.

Almost every time I was there I saw Mr. Braun and Bertha. Mr. Braun never looked happy to see me, but Bertha always gave me big smiles.

When I wasn't at the health club, I hung around with Andy and Josh. Two nights before the end of vacation we went to a party at Amanda Gluck's house. Everyone was sitting around on the old couches in her rec room, talking and listening to music. Since Amber was sitting alone, I sat down next to her.

"Hi, Amber."

"Hi, Jake." She smiled crookedly.

On the table in front of the couch was a big plastic bowl filled with chips. I picked it up and put it on my lap.

Amber gave me a funny look. "I can't believe how you've changed."

"I know," I said. "Everyone says that."

"How did it happen?"

I couldn't tell the truth, so I said, "I've been exercising super hard."

"I bet you've gotten really strong," she said.

"Oh, yeah. I can bench press four-fifty," I said proudly. "Curl one thirty-five and snatch two seventy-five."

"Can you still tell a joke?" she asked.

"Uh . . ." It had been a while since I'd done that, and I wasn't sure. "I guess I could."

"Would you tell me one?" she asked. "I could use a laugh."

"Sure," I said. I thought for a few moments. "How come the chicken crossed the road?"

"I don't know, why?" Amber smiled in anticipation. I remembered how much I used to love her smile.

"To get to the other side," I said.

The smile slowly faded from her face. "That's it?"

I nodded.

"But that's the oldest joke in the world," she said.

"Really? Hmmmm . . . okay, how about this? What's got four wheels and flies?"

"A garbage truck," Amber groaned.

"Wow!" I gasped. "How'd you know?"

Amber gazed at me in disbelief. "Are you *serious*?"

"Sure," I said. "That was my best joke."

Amber studied me with a wistful look. Then she started to get up.

"Where you going?" I asked.

"To the kitchen," she said.

"Can I come too?"

"Why don't you wait here?" she said. "I'll be right back."

So I sat on the couch and ate the chips. Pretty soon I'd emptied the entire bowl. It seemed like Amber was gone for an awful long time. Then Andy and Josh came over.

"Hey, big guy," Josh said, "what's up?"

"I'm waiting for Amber," I said.

"Why?" Andy frowned.

"She went to the kitchen. She said she'd be right back."

"When was that?" Josh asked.

"Well, a pretty long time ago, actually."

"I bet," Andy said. "Amber and a bunch of kids went outside to have a snowball fight about forty-five minutes ago."

"Really? I wonder why she didn't tell me."

Josh and Andy shared a somber look. Then Andy said, "Hey, Jake, why don't you get your jacket? Maybe you, Josh, and me should take a walk."

36

We went outside. Snow blanketed the ground. It was dark and cold. White vapor curled from our lips as we walked. Across the street Amber and a bunch of kids were yelling and laughing as they threw snowballs at each other.

I stopped and watched Amber. I still couldn't understand why she'd left me on the couch waiting all that time.

"Hey, come on, dude." Andy gave me a nudge. He, Josh, and I started to walk toward town. We passed streetlights and houses glittering with Christmas decorations. For a while, no one said anything.

Then Andy said, "Listen, Jake, there's something we want to talk to you about."

"Yeah, I know," I said. "I've gotten really dumb."

Josh winced. "It's not like we think it's your fault or anything."

"Remember when I said that people with huge

muscles can't be that smart because their brains don't have room?" Andy asked.

"I thought that was a joke," I said.

"So did I," said Andy.

"Now we're not so sure," Josh said. "You've gotten totally dumb. Meanwhile, Mr. Braun is going around in your body talking about philosophy."

"I'll bet that three weeks ago he couldn't even *spell* philosophy," added Andy.

"But I really *like* this body," I said. "I mean, having muscles like these is every guy's dream, isn't it?"

Josh and Andy shared a glance and didn't answer. We got into town and headed into the ice cream place. No matter how cold it got, a vanilla cone with chocolate sprinkles still sounded good.

The ice cream place was a big hangout for dirtbags and headbangers. So we weren't surprised to turn the corner and find Barry Dunn coming toward us.

As soon as he saw us, Dunn spun around and took off down a dark side street.

"Wow, you've really got The Dunce freaked!" Josh said with a delighted laugh.

As we walked into the ice cream place, everyone stared at me. But I was used to that, and kind of liked it. I got a vanilla cone with sprinkles and went to look for a table. Josh and Andy were still at the counter, trying different ice cream samples.

They usually took forever to make up their minds.

I found a table near the door and sat down. The ice cream place was lined with windows. Outside I saw a familiar face pass on the sidewalk. It was Bertha, and when she saw me she stopped and smiled.

A second later she came in. "Here alone?"

"My friends are still deciding what to order." I pointed over at the counter.

"I like a man who can make up his mind," Bertha said. "Mind if I sit?"

"No." I didn't really want her to, but it was wrong to be impolite.

"I'm glad we're finally alone," Bertha said, sweeping some strands of blond hair away from her face. "There's something really important I need to say."

I licked the sprinkles off my ice cream and waited.

"Do you mind if I ask how old you are?" she said.

"Uh, fourteen."

"I'm nineteen," Bertha said. "We're five years apart. You probably think that's a lot, right?"

I nodded.

"But when I'm thirty and you're twenty-five, it won't seem like that much," she said.

"Uh, if you say so." I wondered what she was getting at.

Bertha put her elbows on the table and leaned

toward me. The table creaked. I wondered if it was going to break.

"Jake," she said with a wondrous gaze, "do you realize how *special* you are?"

I shook my head.

"If you're built like this at the age of fourteen, do you have *any* idea what you're going to look like at twenty-five?"

"Uh, Arnold Schwarzenegger?" I guessed.

Bertha laughed. "Jake, you're going to make Arnold Schwarzenegger look like a ninety-pound weakling!"

Wow! It was hard to imagine Arnold Schwarzenegger as a shrimp.

"You're going to be like . . ." Bertha couldn't seem to find the word.

"The Incredible Hulk?" I guessed.

"Yes!" Bertha's eyes had a glittery, lively look, and her voice was filled with excitement. "I love men with huge muscles. I know it's not fair to Teddy, but I can't help myself. You're the one for me, Jake."

"Ahem." Someone cleared their throat. Bertha and I looked up. Andy was standing at the table. "I hope I'm not interrupting."

"Oh, of course not." Bertha got up and winked at me. "See you soon, Jake."

Instead of leaving, she went over to the counter. I guess she decided to have some ice cream. Josh and Andy sat down with me.

"What was *that* all about?" Andy whispered.

"Uh, I'm not really sure," I whispered back.

"Well, what did she *say*?" Josh whispered.

"She said it wasn't fair to Teddy, but I'm the one for her."

"Lucky you." Andy smirked.

"She said when she's thirty and I've twenty-five it won't be a big deal," I said. "She said I'll be like the Incredible Hulk."

"And who will she be?" Josh asked with a wink. "Jabba the Hut?"

"Still think it's so great to be big and strong?" Andy asked.

"You can eat more pizza," I said.

Andy groaned. We finished our ice cream. As we went out the door, Bertha caught my eye. She was sitting by herself at a table, eating the biggest ice cream sundae I'd ever seen. The way she gestured at me made it pretty obvious that she hoped I'd ditch my friends and come back later.

Outside in the dark we turned down a snowy side street, taking a shortcut back to our neighborhood.

"I hate to say it, but I'm almost ready to go back to school," Andy said.

"Yeah, just hanging around everyday gets to be a drag," Josh agreed. "Especially when it's cold and you can't do stuff outside."

"How about you, Jake?" Andy asked. "Ready to go to school and get your old body back?"

I shrugged. "I don't know, guys. No matter what you say, I like being big and powerful. I'm not sure I'm ready to give it up."

"Even if it makes you dumb?" Josh asked.

Before I could answer, a bunch of dirtbags stepped into the street in front of us. They were holding baseball bats and ax handles. It looked like they'd been waiting for us. We quickly turned around.

Another bunch appeared behind us.

We were surrounded.

37

Barry Dunn stepped out of the crowd, tapping the head of a baseball bat in his hand.

"It's time for our rematch," he said with a confident sneer. "Now we'll see how tough you *really* are."

The gang of dirtbags moved closer until they formed a circle around Josh, Andy, and me. There was no way to escape. They had baseball bats and ax handles. We had our bare hands.

"Any last words?" Dunn asked.

"Let my friends go," I said. "They have nothing to do with this."

Dunn squinted suspiciously. "Is this another one of your tricks?"

I shook my head. "It's no trick. I just don't want them to get hurt."

"Aw, isn't that sweet?" Dunn leered. "Jake's worried about his friends."

"I actually think it's really considerate of him," Josh said.

"And he happens to be right," added Andy. "We really *don't* have anything to do with this."

"You'd really desert your friend in his hour of need?" Dunn asked them.

"Uh . . ." Andy swallowed and looked around at the dirtbags. "Basically, yes."

"Okay, you two can go," Dunn said.

Josh and Andy turned to me with apologetic expressions on their faces.

"Hope you don't mind, Jake," Josh said. "It's just that baseball bats can hurt."

"But we'll still be your friends," said Andy.

"*If* you live through this," added Josh.

I just nodded. Can't say I blamed them for not wanting to stick around.

"So, uh, we'll call you in the morning, okay?" Andy started to back away.

"If you're not home, we'll try the hospital," added Josh.

The ring of dirtbags parted to let them through. Then it closed again. Dunn was still tapping the head of the bat against his palm.

"And you thought all you needed was big muscles," he sneered.

A few friends who weren't chicken would help, I thought.

"So?" Dunn said.

"So . . . what?" I asked.

"I'm waiting for you to try some kind of trick,"

Dunn said. "That's what you always did in the past."

I shook my head. "Can't think of one this time."

Dunn studied me skeptically for a moment, but I guess he believed me.

"See? It takes more than big muscles," he said. "You were probably better off with a brain."

"I'll try to remember that," I said.

"Actually, you ain't gonna remember anything," Barry growled. He raised his bat as if he was getting ready to hit a baseball. The other dirtbags raised their bats and ax handles. I braced myself. This wasn't going to be pretty.

38

"Hold it, Dunn," a voice said.

Everyone turned. Mr. Braun, with my body, was strolling down the street toward us. His hands were in the pockets of his coat and he didn't seem to be in any particular hurry.

"Get lost," Dunn warned him. "This has nothing to do with you."

"I know that," Mr. Braun said. "I was on my way to meet my girlfriend. I just stopped to show you something."

Barry frowned. "Like what?"

Mr. Braun walked through the crowd of dirt-bags and stopped in front of Dunn. On the other side of the street, Josh and Andy paused on the sidewalk and watched.

"I just noticed the way you were holding the bat," Mr. Braun said.

"What about it?" Dunn asked.

"It's not the correct stance."

"Correct stance?" Dunn scowled. "What are you

talking about? This ain't baseball, it's a fight."

"Doesn't matter," Mr. Braun said. "If you're going to hit a baseball, a softball, or Sherman's head, there's only one way to hold the bat. Look."

Pretending he was holding a bat in his hand, Mr. Braun got into a stance. "See this? Hands together. Elbows out. The bat back. Weight on the back foot."

Dunn tried to mimic the position.

"No, no." Mr. Braun shook his head. "You have to hold the bat farther back. Otherwise, you wind up swinging backward before you swing forward. Here, look."

Mr. Braun reached for Barry's bat. "It's like this. You hold the bat way back here. Get it?"

Dunn nodded.

"Good," Mr. Braun said, handing the bat to me and turning to the rest of gang. "Now all of you, get into the proper stance."

The others tried to follow Mr. Braun's instructions.

"No, no!" Mr. Braun went around shaking his head and correcting them. Then he turned to Andy and Josh. "Kent, Hopka. You guys know how to hold a bat. Come over here and show them."

The next thing I knew, Mr. Braun, Josh, and Andy were holding baseball bats, and showing the dirtbags the correct stance. I still had Dunn's bat.

"There, do you all get it?" Mr. Braun asked.

The dirtbags nodded.

"Good." Mr. Braun raised his bat and motioned for Josh, Andy, and me to do the same. "Now I'll give you to the count of three to get out of here before me and Hopka and Kent and Sherman beat you into greasy grimy gopher guts."

A stunned silence descended over the gang of dirtbags. Some of them still had bats and ax handles, but now, instead of facing one unarmed person, they were facing four of us with bats.

Barry Dunn's jaw dropped. "Why, you . . . !"

Mr. Braun turned to him. "I've had it with you, Dunn. The next time you so much as touch a kid, on or off school grounds . . . the next time I even *hear* that you've bothered someone, I'm going to come after you, understand?"

Dunn nodded slowly. Mr. Braun turned to the rest of the dirtbags. "That goes for all of you, too. Now, get lost."

Muttering angrily, Barry and his friends trudged away down the street. Mr. Braun turned to Josh, Andy, and me and smiled. "Funny what can happen when you use your brain, huh?"

39

The day after vacation, I got to Mr. Dirksen's room half an hour before the first bell. Mr. Dirksen and Mr. Braun were already there. Mr. Dirksen was bent over the experiment, fiddling with some wires. Mr. Braun was sitting on a school desk. His shoulders were slumped and the corners of his mouth hung down.

"Hey, Mr. Braun, what's up?" I asked.

He didn't answer. He just sat there looking glum.

"Something wrong?" I asked.

"Bertha broke up with me last night," he said. "She said she needed someone with bigger muscles. I tried to explain that I'd be getting mine back, but she didn't believe me."

"Bummer, Mr. Braun," I said. "Sorry about that."

The gym teacher nodded. "It's probably for the best. Even when I get my old body back, I don't think I'll be the same person."

"Me, neither," I said.

Mr. Braun brightened. "You think you and your friends will take better care of your bodies from now on?"

"No, but we'll probably try badminton."

Mr. Braun grinned. I grinned too.

"Okay, gentlemen," Mr. Dirksen said. "We're ready."

I stepped over to my spot and Mr. Braun went to his. I knew I was going to miss having his body, but I was looking forward to having brains again. I glanced over at Mr. Braun and caught his eye.

"Being really smart was kind of fun," he said.

"It's not an all-or-none proposition," I said. "You can work on your brains."

"And you can work on your body," he said. "You don't have to be a muscle man, but you should cut down on the junk food and get in shape."

"Here goes!" Mr. Dirksen said.

Whhuuummmppp!

40

That afternoon, Amber and I walked down the hall toward the gym.

"So how do you stop a two-thousand pound elephant from charging?" I asked.

"I don't know, how?" Amber said.

"Take away its credit cards."

Amber smiled and gazed affectionately at me. "I still can't believe the change in you, Jake. Just a week ago, you were a muscleheaded dimwit."

"They weren't really muscles," I explained. "I was just all swollen up. It was an allergic reaction to something I'd eaten. And the reason I seemed so dim was because of the medication they had me on."

It was a totally feeble explanation, but people seemed to buy it just the same. How else could they explain what had happened to me?

"Well, I'm glad you're the old Jake again," Amber said.

"Hey, you guys, wait up!" someone yelled. We

turned and saw Josh and Andy jogging up the hall toward us.

"So, I see the swelling went down," Andy said.

"How about the swelled head?" Josh asked.

"Very funny," I grumbled.

"Hey, just kidding." Josh held out a small bag of chips. "Want some?"

I hesitated. After all, I'd promised Mr. Braun I'd cut down on the junk food.

Then again, it was just a couple of chips . . . I reached in and got a handful of chiplets.

"Hey! Just one!" Josh cried.

"Naw, it's okay." Andy slapped me on the back. "It's good to know that *some* things never change."

About the Author

Todd Strasser has written many award-winning novels for young and teenage readers. Among his best known books are *Help! I'm Trapped in My Teacher's Body*; *Help! I'm Trapped in Obedience School*; and *Abe Lincoln for Class President!* Todd speaks frequently at schools about the craft of writing and conducts writing workshops for young people. He works out at a gym near his home, but hasn't grown big muscles yet.